THE LAST DROP

A Table for Two Novella

LAYLA REYNE

About This Book

A cocktail you won't forget ...

Ingredients:
One down-on-his-luck chef struggling to make it in his
hometown.
One nomadic bartender allergic to putting down roots.
A hot and heavy night in the Big Easy that neither of them
can stop thinking about.

Directions:
Pour ingredients into the chef's final hope, a queer-friendly
gastropub in New Orleans.
Set a timer for how long the bartender is willing to lend his
skills.
Let ingredients meld as they build a concept for their
community, share drinks and menus, and learn to expand
their horizons from right at home.

Stir until the two can no longer be separated and love is guaranteed.

Sip this short and spicy M/M workplace romance novella for a light and easy happy hour treat.

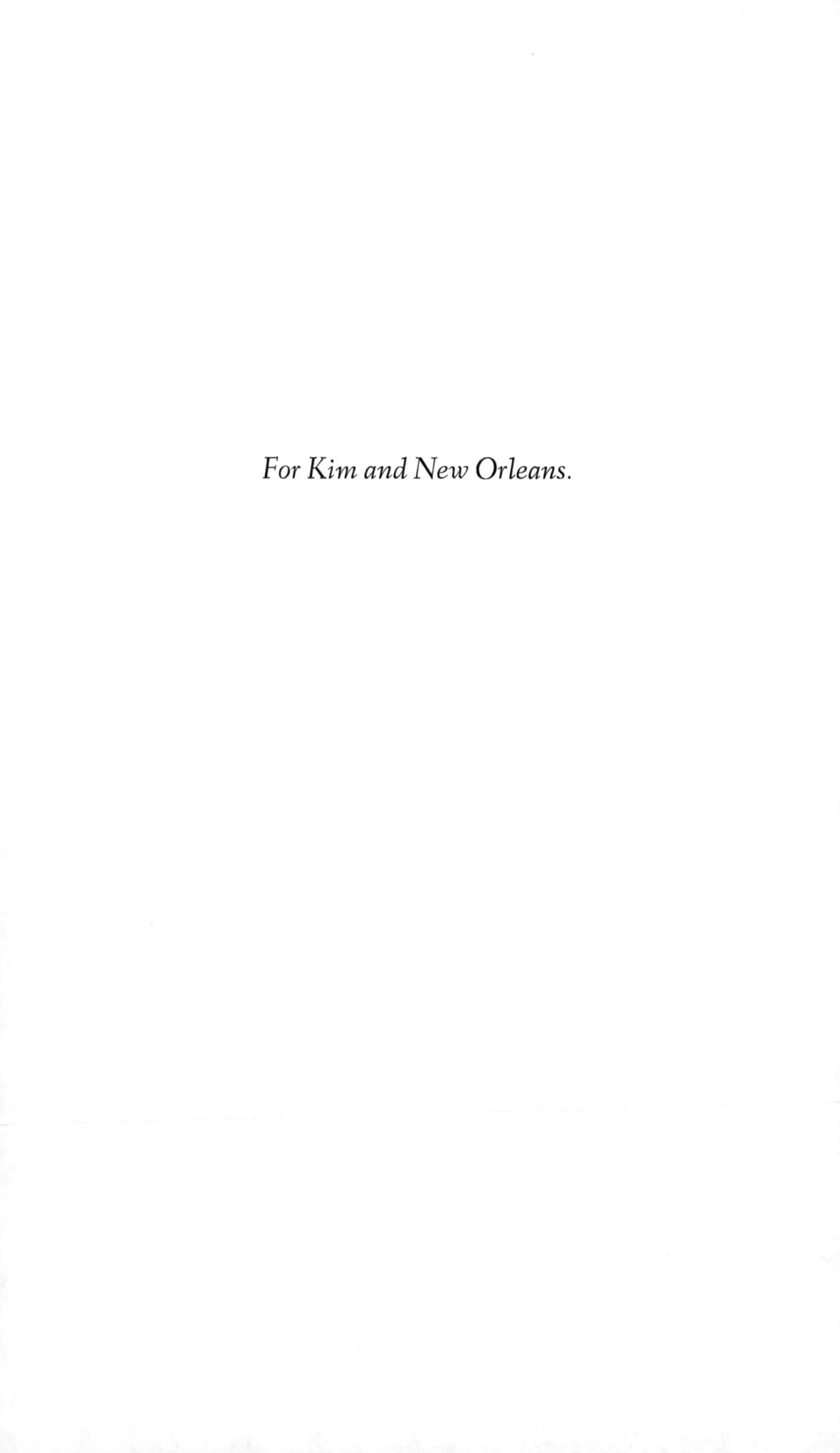

For Kim and New Orleans.

Chapter One

Dear Mr. Manhattan,
We met nine months ago at a bar in New Orleans. You were
the too cute hipster behind the bar. I was the out-of-work
chef acting the Virgin Mary with my too big hands. You
blew my mind with your cocktails, then you rocked my
world and started it spinning again. I've got a gig for you.
Dram, Bywater, New Orleans. Come drink with me.
Yours, Mr. New Orleans

Three strikes and you're out, according to baseball and
conventional wisdom, neither of which Greg Valteau liked
all that much. If he believed in that kind of nonsense, he
would have never gone to culinary school, never made a
hollandaise that didn't break, never bought the fucking
Saints jersey on his back. He believed in ghosts and

vampires more than he believed in some three strikes bullshit.

But something about tonight felt different. Felt final.

He'd known it would be tough. More restaurants failed than succeeded, and New Orleans itself was a challenge. While things were better now in his hometown, it had taken time to bounce back after Katrina. He'd hoped to be a part of the vibrant re-awakening. Instead, he had three failed concepts and a pair of very callused hands to show for all his efforts, for the heart he'd poured back into his city only to have his dreams washed out into the Gulf.

Maybe it was time to pack it up and go back to New York or join his best friend in the Bay Area. Except as much as his heart ached to be with him, it ached even worse at the thought of leaving his hometown again. He was committed to the humidity, the mosquitos, to his family here, and to the soulful culture he loved, that was a part of him. But making that commitment work with the part of his soul that also wanted to cook for a living was fucking hard.

"What can I get you to drink?"

Greg looked up from his empty hands and blinked, twice. He didn't normally go for hipster, but *damn*. The Mohawk of black curls, the amber eyes fringed by thick lashes, and the trim dark beard worked for the bartender. As did the fitted gray vest, mint-green dress shirt, and tight black jeans, all showcasing a compact, fit body, and... just, *damn*.

Talk about hard; Greg had to shift on his stool.

The bartender tilted his head and bit his plump

bottom lip. Not making things any less hard for Greg. Neither did the much-missed accent that blanketed the bartender's words when he spoke. "Judging by that look on your face a moment ago," he said, "I'd say something heavy on the alcohol and light on everything else." Clipped as the thick New York accent was, Greg would lay odds on Manhattan.

"Was I that obvious?"

"Well, you were doing your best Virgin Mary impression." He struck a palms-up pose, and Greg half groaned, half laughed. He hoped he hadn't looked quite so woeful. Mr. Manhattan winked and slid a napkin in front of Greg. "I promise, all is not lost."

"How many times have you made that promise tonight?"

He shrugged a shoulder. "Half a dozen. Doesn't make it any less true." He flipped an old-fashioned tumbler right side up and dropped a giant sphere of ice into the glass. "And I know just the drink for you."

Over the ice, he poured Sazerac, cognac, and sweet vermouth, and Greg smiled. He had a pretty good idea where this was headed, and he was impressed at the bartender's confidence. Pouring the cocktail freehand, he added a shot of Bénédictine, then dashes of Peychaud's and Angostura bitters. "By that accent and the Saints jersey," the man said as he spiral shaved a lemon rind, "I'm guessing you're local." He swirled the mixture with the rind, dropped it into the glass, then set the drink on Greg's napkin. "So I know you'll appreciate this."

Greg picked up the glass and held the cocktail under

his nose, eyes fluttering closed. The familiar rye and herbal notes stung his nostrils, only to be smoothed over by the wave of underlying sweetness. Home in a glass. "Vieux Carré," he said, letting the words he'd learned as a kid roll off his tongue, the inflection perfected in culinary school and the best French kitchens in New York. He opened his eyes again to a pair of heated amber ones. Gazes locked, Greg tipped the glass against his lips and sipped.

Fucking perfect.

He took another swallow, savoring the spicy-sweet cocktail as it washed over his tongue and down his throat, then he ran his tongue along his bottom lip to catch any drops he'd missed.

"Guessing by your accent," he said to the blushing bartender, "you're not local, but I wouldn't know it from this." He lifted his glass in praise. "Nice job, Mr. Manhattan."

Blushing pink gave way to a deeper red, paired with a lovely pleased smile. "How's a guy from New Orleans recognize a Manhattan accent?"

"Chef'ed in the City."

"Anywhere I'd know?"

Greg shrugged a shoulder, same as Manhattan had done earlier, and hid his smile behind another sip from his glass.

Manhattan's answering laugh sent a spike of heat zinging down Greg's spine, straight to his dick. "Big shot then," the bartender said. "Why'd you leave?"

"Because this"—Greg waved a hand toward the ornate bar, toward the jazz band on stage, then rattled the ice ball in his glass—"is home." He finished his drink with a satisfied hum, and as he did, curiosity and all those detective shows he compulsively watched tempted him to ask, "How does a handsome guy from Manhattan make a Vieux Carré so well?"

"Was one of the first drinks I learned to make," he answered. "Dad didn't have any mixers in the house."

What did they say about curiosity and the cat? Flirtatious mood killed, Greg was torn between making an apology and asking more questions he shouldn't, but Manhattan's face didn't betray any melancholy or bitterness. Just a statement of fact delivered with a bemused smile.

"Learned some other tricks too." He pushed a cocktail menu across the bar. "Take a look. Decide what you want to try next."

While Manhattan worked the other end of the bar, Greg perused the menu. Old reliables—Hurricane, Sazerac, Margarita—but each with a unique spin, and other drinks from regions near and far. Eclectic mixes of flavors that spoke to a certain hipster's big palette and big ideas.

Greg's mind spun, falling into the familiar game he and his best friend used to play when they worked in kitchens together, guessing the who, what, when, where, and why of their diners. Only tonight, Greg was speculating about the bartender who was headed back his direction.

"What'll it be?"

"Balcones Bomb." Greg's affinity for corn soup had

drawn him to the cocktail made with the pure corn bourbon from Texas.

One corner of Manhattan's mouth hitched up. "Good choice." He set about making the cocktail—freehand again—pouring the Balcones whisky and other ingredients into a shaker with ice.

"How long you been doing this?" Greg asked.

"Going on seven years." He gave the shaker a few vigorous pumps, then set it aside and retrieved a martini glass. Into the glass, he poured a splash of chili oil and swirled it around, coating the sides of the glass before pitching the liquid into the sink.

"Here in New Orleans?" Greg didn't think so. Skills and looks like his, word would have gotten around the restaurant crowd.

"No, I've only been here a few months." He uncapped the shaker, fitted on a strainer, and poured the liquid into the glass, finishing it with a sprig of thyme. He pushed it across the bar to Greg. "Enjoy."

One sip and Greg almost came in his jeans. He was a chef after all, and right behind food and sex on his ecstasy ladder was a good drink. And this was the best chilled corn soup he'd ever had but in cocktail form. Fucking hell. He had to have this man, in his bed and in his next restaurant, whenever that happened. "Keep making drinks like this and you'll make a name for yourself here in no time."

"Afraid I won't be around long enough for that."

Fucking hell again. And yet, not all that surprising. His hometown tended to attract the nomadic sort. If Greg didn't have his roots here, he'd probably go too at this point, not keep fighting this damn hard to make it work. But for all his moping, there was no debate for him.

Didn't sound like there was much debate for Mr. Manhattan either. He was leaving soon, but he was here now. Maybe Greg could get one of the things he wanted. He caught the bartender's attention the next time he passed close, and Greg tilted forward on the stool, lowering his voice. "You around long enough after work tonight for me to fuck you?"

Tony tried his hardest to ignore the excitement and anticipation that kept sneaking up on him. That made his breath quicken, his blood race, and his dick swell. New Orleans—the man, who'd paid in cash so Tony still didn't know his name—was waiting outside. Waiting to walk him home and take him to bed. The night ahead promised the chef's big body atop his, his big rough hands roaming Tony's body, stroking his dick... Failing to ignore. Tony shook his head, chasing away the fantasy and focusing on his closing to-do list.

The manager had already emptied the register of cash and receipts, the servers were straightening the dining area, and the kitchen staff had mostly cleared out. He just had to take care of the bar. Glasses and utensils into the dishwasher. Rinse, dry, and cap the taps. Date the wine bottles. Rinse the drains. Shine the bar top. Mop the backbar. Down to just the trash on his list, Tony shimmied the bin out from under the bar and set it on the other side of the flip for the servers to toss any trash into. He washed his hands and did his final departing pat-down check, making sure he had everything: wallet, tips, keys, phone.

"You guys all set?" he called to the servers.

"We're good," one of them replied. "Go bang that tiger waiting for you outside."

Excitement and anticipation crested once more, as did curiosity. "Tiger?"

The server slapped his outer shoulder. "Tattoo of a tiger. LSU alum, if I had to guess."

Tony would have to get a closer look. He wondered if the handsome chef had more ink. Didn't they all these days?

He exited out the back door and turned right, intending to circle around to the front and meet New Orleans there, but a voice called from the opposite direction.

"How's a guy from Manhattan end up in New Orleans?"

Of course the chef would know to wait for him here; restaurant staff rarely came and went out the front door. Tony turned and admired the man leaning against the brick wall. He was every bit as gorgeous here as he had been sitting at the bar, even more so in the halo of the alley lights. Warm brown skin, dark soulful eyes, long legs and a built upper body, and a sexy as hell grin, tonight's earlier despair wiped away by a parade of cocktails. He pushed off the wall and swaggered toward Tony, and the way he moved his big body with such grace, such confidence, was sexy as hell too.

"You gonna answer, *Manhattan*?"

Tony should really ask his name, but he liked the nickname bestowed on him too much to let the anonymity go. New Orleans wasn't asking either; he seemed like a nickname kind of guy. And circumstances being what they were, this could only be a one-night stand. Anonymity was better. Kinder. As would be an answer to New Orleans's question. He would better understand in the morning and hopefully not take it personally.

"I wandered my way down," Tony said. "DC, Virginia Beach, Charleston, Mobile."

He grinned wider. "You like the water?"

More like he didn't do landlocked. He'd lasted a month in Atlanta, then hightailed it to Mobile. He needed the ocean, needed to know he wasn't trapped. Guilt squeezed his heart, threatening a wave of memories. He focused on the man in front of him instead, cutting through the breakers. "I do," he answered simply, hoping to move this along.

But the tiger was a curious one. "Why'd you leave the City?"

"The City," Tony echoed, in the same enamored tone New Orleans had used.

"You loved it too," he rightly surmised.

"Always will," Tony answered. "It's home." In a way no place else ever would be, in a way he didn't want any other place to be. Easier to keep moving. "I wanted to see more." He closed the distance between them and splayed a hand over New Orleans's chest, fingertips digging lightly into packed muscle. "I want to see more of what's under here too."

The chef inhaled, bit his bottom lip, and laid a hand on Tony's hip, nudging him closer. Tony went eagerly, and New Orleans drifted his hand over Tony's ass, hauling him closer. The same anticipation that had been riding Tony all night had clearly been riding New Orleans too. The other man's cock pressed against Tony's thigh was thick and hard. Tony bit back a groan. It escaped, however, when New Orleans lowered his face and scraped his trimmed goatee across Tony's cheek, the scruff-to-scruff friction insane. Tony clutched a fistful of cotton, and a gravelly laugh rumbled out of the man pressed against him.

"Where's home for you now?" he asked.

Two questions wrapped up in one. The answer to either wouldn't be the same tomorrow, but for tonight, home was thankfully close. "Two blocks over, three streets down." He rocked his hips and shifted his thigh, pressing more firmly against New Orleans and eliciting a gasp. He could play this game too.

"Short walk."

Tony flattened his hand over the chef's chest, rubbing over the nipple that puckered under his touch. "How about you take it with me so we can get out of these clothes and onto the promised fucking?"

"Goddamn, I fucking want that." New Orleans rocked his hips with more force and nipped at Tony's neck. "Want you."

Gasping, Tony drew out of the other man's arms before he came in his fucking pants. The only way he wanted to come tonight was with a certain chef's big rough hand around his dick. He turned toward the alley exit and leered over his shoulder, shaking his ass a little for good, tortured measure. He held out a hand. "You coming with me?"

"Oh, baby, more than once if I have anything to say about it." He swaggered forward and slipped his hand into Tony's. "Lead the way, Manhattan."

A random hookup on his last night here probably wasn't the smartest move, but the hot, hungry look in New Orleans's eyes was undeniable. As was the way he used Tony's hand in his to move Tony in front of him, then looped his other arm around Tony's chest and crowded close behind him, his hands roaming Tony's front and his dick grazing Tony's ass with every step they took together. A promise of the night ahead. Tony let the excitement and anticipation wash over him, not ignoring it any longer. He couldn't think of a better send off.

Chapter Two

It was a short walk from the bar to the shotgun double where Manhattan was staying. Though walk was being generous; stumble was more accurate. Between the creative cocktails Greg had continued to consume and, once they'd left the alley behind the bar, his need to run his hands all over Manhattan's tight, hot body, Greg hadn't been overly concerned with putting one foot in front of the other.

"I don't normally go for hipster." He nipped at Manhattan's neck as the other man fumbled his front door keys. "But the body under this getup." He slipped free the last button of Manhattan's vest and spread his hands over his chest.

"Fuck," Manhattan groaned as he dropped his head back onto Greg's shoulder.

Taking advantage of all the skin on display, Greg licked into the crook of Manhattan's neck and lapped up a night's worth of sweat and lingering bergamot soap. Could they fuck right here on the porch? It was three in the morning. No one would see.

Seemed Manhattan had the same idea. He thrust out his chest and thrust back his ass. "Want to feel those hands on me."

Greg ran them in opposite directions, one south to cup Manhattan through his jeans, the other north to lightly grasp the base of his throat. "You like these?"

He groaned louder. "Didn't think a chef's hands got like that."

"I live and die by my cast iron skillets." He curled his fingers over the ridge of Manhattan's cock, hardening behind the denim, and with his other hand, teased the thrumming pulse point in his neck. "And after Katrina, we all had to be carpenters. These hands have built three restaurants from the inside out."

"You've got three restaurants?"

"Nah, man, three flops." He brought his hands back to Manhattan's middle and began working open his dress shirt. "But that's not what I want to talk about tonight. Want to talk about getting you out of these clothes, then getting inside you."

"Get in the house, New Orleans, and you can talk all you want."

Greg liked the sound of that. Liked the sound of the key flipping the lock even better. Manhattan opened the door, and Greg pushed them over the threshold. They stumbled, a tangled mass of half-stripped limbs, toward the foyer wall, and at the last second, Greg braced a forearm next to Manhattan's head, saving him from becoming a pancake. At this new angle, Greg had a stellar view of Manhattan's moonlit amber eyes and his heaving chest, sprinkled with curly black hair.

"Okay," the bartender panted through a grin. "Talk now."

Fuck talking.

Fuck everything that didn't involve his mouth on Manhattan's, his tongue diving between Manhattan's full lips, the moan he swallowed and echoed back, the taste of hazelnut and berries from the last cocktail of the night. And of something else smoky and fleeting Greg couldn't put a finger on. He'd get a whiff of it, and then it was gone. He chased after it again and again, his tongue searching every corner of Manhattan's mouth, his fingers raking through the springy hair on his chest, his body seeking out heat and friction.

Until Greg needed more air than he was snatching between kisses. He wrenched his mouth away with a muttered, "Fuck," and rested his forehead in the crook of Manhattan's neck.

"Best conversation all night." Manhattan cupped the back of Greg's head, fingers rubbing over the short coarse hairs. Greg wanted to nuzzle into the touch. "Maybe all week."

Other parts of them wanted to converse too, most notably their cocks, which were each testing the fortitude of denim. Greg dropped a hand again to the bartender's crotch and skated fingers along his dick. "Maybe let's move this to the bedroom."

"Agreed." Manhattan leaned his head back, meeting

Greg's gaze, and his smirk was pure sex. "Condoms and lube are in there too."

"Jesus Christ." Greg dove for his mouth again, chasing away the evil grin, until Manhattan slipped his hold and flipped a light switch.

Good thing, as Greg would have likely tripped over the moving boxes in the dark. "You weren't kidding. You're on the move again? Soon?"

"On to the next adventure."

"Where's that?" Greg followed him through the living room and kitchen, toward the bedroom in the back. The furniture, covered in sheets, must have come with the rental. The couple of boxes per room, Greg guessed, were personal items Manhattan would take with him. A car's worth at most.

"Wherever I decide to stop," Manhattan said. "Never the same place twice." He stood over the threshold from bathroom to bedroom, resting back against the doorjamb as he loosened his jeans and toed off his shoes. He was a debauched sight to behold. Vest, shirt, and pants hanging open, cock hard, lips swollen and cheeks red, all that black hair askew.

Greg closed the distance between them, yanked the vest and shirt down and off his arms, then shoved a hand inside his pants. Beneath Manhattan's briefs, his cock was stiff and dripping. Greg growled as he swiped his fingers over the tip, gathering moisture then stroking the impressive length. "Shame I only get one night with you." Another stroke. "With this."

The body against his, the cock in his hand, surged forward, begging for more. "Better make it count."

One more stroke, then Greg moved his hand off Manhattan's dick and over his hip. "You got a mattress still?" He palmed an ass cheek before sliding his hand under Manhattan's thigh and hiking it up over his own hip, giving Greg access to the place he wanted most. "Or I can fuck you against this wall here. Or on the floor." He circled a finger around Manhattan's rim. "As long as I get my dick inside this hole."

Manhattan shuddered one second, then was in Greg's arms the next, jumping up and wrapping his legs around Greg's waist. "Mattress, in there." He nodded toward the room. "Go."

Hands full of ass cheeks, Greg toed off his own shoes, then spun and entered the bedroom. That enigmatic thing he couldn't put his finger on slapped him in the face—charred oak. A pony-sized whiskey barrel sat on the bedside table.

"Whatcha' got in there?" Greg asked as he put a knee, then Manhattan's back to the mattress.

"Manhattan."

Greg laughed out loud. "You don't say?"

The handsome man smiled up at him, amber eyes twinkling. "Reminds me of home."

"Tell me about it," Greg said as he scooted back off the bed, taking Manhattan's jeans and briefs with him. "The drink," he clarified. He'd noticed Manhattan's earlier dodges, and the last thing he wanted was to throw this night off course.

Especially as the bartender's swollen cock bounced free. It was all Greg could do not to pounce. But if he only had one night with this beautiful man, he was going to fucking savor it, like the best meal of his life. He dropped his own pants and underwear, yanked his shirt off over his head, and grinned as Manhattan gave in and stroked his cock. Greg crawled back onto the bed between his legs. "What exactly did you use?"

"Black Maple Hill..." Manhattan's breath caught as Greg lifted one leg, rested it on his shoulder, and whorled a tongue around the knot of his ankle. "For the rye."

Greg slid his hand down a firm calf dusted with dark hair, over a smooth inner thigh and into the groove where leg met groin, then danced his fingertips over Manhattan's balls. "And the vermouth?"

"Antica," he gutted out, three syllables of keening want.

Greg left the leg on his shoulder, then lifted the other one, repeating his teasing motions. "The bitters?"

Pale skin flushed, Manhattan arched his back. "Peychaud's. Seemed appropriate."

When he reached his balls this time, Greg upped the ante and gave them a firm squeeze. "Nothing about this is appropriate, baby."

"Fuck, New Orleans, those hands." His back hit the mattress, chest heaving like he'd run a marathon. "Just fucking fuck me. Please."

Greg chuckled. "Oh, I will, don't you worry." Taking an ankle in each hand, he coasted his grip over calves, behind knees, to the backs of Manhattan's thighs, pushing them back and wide. "Anything else in that barrel?" He bent and ran his tongue up the length of Manhattan's cock. "A secret ingredient?" He circled the tip. "Like that splash of chili oil in the cocktail earlier tonight."

"Luxardo." Pant. "Maraschino." Pant. "Wash." Then a tortured whimper when Greg dipped lower and blew hot breath on his hole. "Oh fuck."

Flattening his tongue, Greg made one, then because the smell and taste and flutter were so damn intoxicating, another pass around Manhattan's rim. "You gonna leave the keg or take it with you?"

"Keep doing that and you can have it to remember me by."

Greg spread his legs wider and licked up the crease of his balls. "Don't think I'm gonna have any trouble remembering this sort of perfection."

Perfection he finally gave into, spreading his hands and pressing Manhattan's legs toward the mattress, causing an arch in his back and a thrust of his gorgeous cock toward Greg. Bowing, Greg met the bodily plea, his and Manhattan's, and closed his lips around Manhattan's cock and took him in farther, until Greg's nose was buried in wiry black hair.

Above him, Manhattan groaned and tossed his head on the pillow. Greg skirted his hands down, fingers framing Manhattan's balls then teasing his taint while Greg's thumbs worked him open. Because for all his focus on savoring, on making this good for Manhattan, Greg was close to the edge already, his cock painfully hard and dripping down his thigh.

A hand palmed his scalp, and Greg realized he'd closed

his eyes. He looked up into Manhattan's beseeching gold ones. "Please fuck me," he begged. "I want you inside me, your hand around my cock, when I come."

Greg released his cock with a salacious pop. "Goddamn, you're perfect."

And perfectly prepared. "Good thing I hadn't packed these." He tossed a condom and lube toward Greg, who reared back on his haunches, rolled on the condom, and slicked up his cock. Manhattan's eyes became impossibly more hooded, amber slits of burning desire. "Fuck yes, get that inside me."

Falling forward, Greg planted one hand on the pillow beside Manhattan's head while the other guided his cock to his entrance. He pushed in, slow and easy, savoring the heat and warmth that grabbed hold and wouldn't let go.

Of more than just his cock. "Jesus Christ," he cursed again. "You feel so good."

Even better when Manhattan curled a hand around his neck and brought them breath to breath, tongue flicking out for a teasing lick of Greg's lips. "Get that big, rough hand on me and get me off. Hard."

Greg didn't have to be told twice. He wrapped his slick hand around Manhattan's cock and stroked him hard with each equally hard snap of his hips. Pounding, jerking, their grunts mirrors of each other, broken only by curses and pleas for "more" and "harder." Until Manhattan's drawn out, guttural "Yes" against Greg's lips preceded a hot gush of come over his fist. Greg came with a final thrust of his hips as he kissed the lovely, talented bartender, deep and claiming, breathing into him the pleasure of the best orgasm Greg had ever experienced.

It was a hazy trip down from the high, motions made heavy and slow by cocktails and sex. Manhattan was moving somewhat easier, taking away the condom Greg tied off and coming back from the bathroom with a warm rag to clean up. Greg was just beginning to doze when a waft of spice and sweet hit his nose. He forced open his eyes to find Manhattan beside him with a shot glass of his namesake drink in hand.

"Better than an after-sex cigarette." He took a sip, then held the shot glass out to Greg, who levered up on one elbow.

It was everything Greg loved about barrel-aged cocktails. So much more complex, the charred oak subtlety rounding off the sharp edges of the rye. "It's fucking perfect." He handed the glass back, then tucked his head under Manhattan's chin, burying his nose in all his tantalizing chest hair. "Just like you."

Manhattan stretched, setting aside the glass, then relaxed into Greg, pulling them both deeper into the bed. "Think you'll remember me?" He coasted a hand over Greg's head, like he'd done before, and Greg nuzzled into it, like he'd wanted to do earlier.

"No doubt," he mumbled, before drifting off to sleep.

When Greg woke in the morning, Manhattan the man was gone, but the barrel remained, a reminder for Greg to savor.

Chapter Three

Summer was still going strong in the Big Easy, and with each muggy day that passed in the march toward September, Greg held his breath and kept an eye on the weather. He'd been working in New York when Katrina had hit, but his family had been here. They still had lingering PTSD from the trauma; so did a lot of people in Greg's hometown. Yes, New Orleans had moved on and thrived, but a heightened sense of anxiety permeated the late summer air. He'd been home long enough now to sense it too. Add to that the restlessness that came whenever he was between projects, and Greg was a ball of nerves. Twice daily trips to French Truck for iced coffee probably didn't help, but the roasted coffee ground with chicory, shaken with sweet cream, and served over ice was an addiction he couldn't shake. At least not until the temps dropped.

Only sex or a kitchen would settle him. The first was swiftly ruled out, even though it had been a month since

Greg's hookup with Mr. Manhattan. He should accept their night for what it was: amazing cocktails, an amazing fuck, and an amazing parting gift. But acknowledging the pony barrel of rye whiskey, sweet vermouth, bitters, and a splash of cherry liquor was the closest he'd ever come to Mr. Manhattan again put a damper on the idea stirring at the back of Greg's mind. It was only a vague notion—so many pieces would have to fall into place—but it was there, adding to the jangle of nerves. And Greg had zero desire to take someone else to bed. The memories of the sexy hipster writhing beneath him were still too fresh. The comparison wouldn't be fair to anyone.

Fuck, he needed to find a kitchen. And at this point in his life and career, there were only two people he could cook with. As one of those was across the country, he snagged his phone and called the closer of the two.

"Gregory," his mother answered, "I was just getting ready to call you."

He lowered the phone, checked the screen, then lifted it back to his ear. "I called Dad."

"Well, you got me. Is that a problem?"

Always with the sass. His mother delivered it daily, at home and on the city council. Greg had learned at a young age that respecting it was the surest path to peace. "No, ma'am."

"Where are you?"

"French Truck in the Quarter."

"Good, you're relatively close. Meet us in the Bywater in fifteen. I'll text you the address."

"Wait!" he called, certain she was halfway to hanging

up, expecting her directive to be obeyed. He would, of course, but he needed some idea where this was headed to mentally prepare himself. "Isn't Dad cooking in the Marigny today?" That's why he'd called in the first place. And unless the shelter volunteer schedule had changed, his dad wasn't in the Bywater until later in the week. "I was calling to see if I could help. Need to get my hands dirty."

"He got things started this morning. Staff there is holding it down until he gets back. You can go with him from here."

"Where's here?"

A moment later, the phone vibrated in his hand.

"Sent you the address," his mom said. "See you soon."

She beat him to the hang up, and Greg lowered the phone to read her text, an address off Dauphine. Fifteen minutes to get there, and if he were a minute late, he'd hear about it. He could make it at a brisk walk, but in this humidity, hell no.

He drained his iced coffee, tossed the cup into the trash, and hustled two blocks to the streetcar. He took it as far as the Marigny, cut through Crescent Park, then up two blocks to Dauphine, dodging the early lunch go-ers at the Bywater's outdoor cafés and forcing himself not to slow and admire the street murals. They always caught his interest whenever he was down here.

He rounded a corner and spied his parents in the distance. His dad stood out of the way in the shadow of a building overhang, fanning himself with a magazine, while his mom, across the sidewalk, leaned against a lamppost, soaking up the sun like she wanted to live on the face of it. He couldn't remember a time when she had ever complained about the heat.

She noticed him first and waved, her white linen sleeve falling back to her elbow and her gold bracelets glinting against brown skin, a shade richer than his and his father's. Greg jogged the last half block, regretting it almost immediately as sweat poured down his back. Also like his dad, he did not have his mother's tolerance for heat. Never had. But he didn't complain; it was worth making it there on time and earning his mother's wide, pleased smile.

A little too pleased, in fact. "What are you up to?" he asked as he embraced her.

"Why do you assume I'm up to something?"

"You didn't call me out here for nothing."

"Well, that's true." She stepped to his side and gestured across the sidewalk to the two-story building his dad leaned against. It's two front windows were papered over, its front entry boarded up, and the unit upstairs appeared empty too. "Look what we found."

"A vacant building?"

His dad pushed off the wall and joined them. "You're burying the lead, Charlene." His dad drew a set of keys out of his pocket. "Which is why I have these. We can let ourselves in the back door and get out of this God-forsaken sun."

She rose on her toes, barely reached his chin for a kiss, and snatched the keys out of his hands. "You're lucky I love you, Henry Valteau." She flounced off around the side of the building, and his dad dutifully followed, laughing.

Greg laughed too, the two of them as prickly and as in love with each other as they had been for forty years. He was lucky to have them, lucky to witness and have their love, and lucky they supported his cooking. It hadn't been easy, but they'd always had his back. He crossed the sidewalk and laid a hand on the boarded-up entry, imagining what was behind it. Excitement fizzed in his belly like prosecco, the bubbles floating up and bursting in his chest. He had an inkling of what was going on here, what his parents had found, but he didn't say anything as he joined them around back, letting them have their moment and tempering his own hopes.

Until he crossed the threshold, walked through the narrow back hallway, past the darkened kitchen, and into the open area at the front of the lower floor space.

He vaguely heard his father's loafers peel off the sticky floor and felt his mother's warm hand on his forearm, but those senses were secondary to sight, smell, and taste. His gaze roamed the large open area, taking in the rotting bar, the crumbling brick walls, and the shaft of rainbow-colored light that streaked through the uncovered corner of stained-glass above the door. He inhaled the lingering smoke, the traces of alcohol, and the ever-present moisture in the decaying wood, drains, and probably also the walls. The soupy, stuffy air bound the ingredients in a cocktail Greg tasted in the back of his throat.

Along with everything this place could be.

The vague notion stirring at the back of his mind returned, taking on a more definite shape as the first piece fell into place. "It's perfect."

"I thought so," his mom smugly agreed.

"*We* thought so." His dad clasped his shoulder. "The building came through one of the brokers I work with. The owner's looking for a new tenant for the commercial space and the residential unit upstairs."

His mom squeezed his arm. "You can work and live here. Like you've always wanted."

He had always wanted that convenience, and he never again wanted the *in*convenience of a griping neighbor. If you lived in a building with a restaurant in New Orleans, you had better learn to live with the smell of boiling seafood. He'd be more than happy to wake up to that comforting smell every morning. Just like he'd be happy to walk downstairs and into his kitchen. His restaurant. It didn't look like much now—looked like less than much, if he were being honest—but the bones were there, and they were beautiful. Here in this vibrant, funky neighborhood, this place could be a home for him and his restaurant. The multi-color light caught his attention again. It could also be a home for the LGBTQ community. He'd been searching for a way to get more involved, to make a difference beyond just helping out at his parents' shelters. This was something *he* could do.

He turned to his dad, who wore the same proud and pleased smile his mother had flashed earlier. "How long can they hold it?" Greg asked. "I need to find an investor." He eyed the bar area again. "And there's someone else I need to get on board."

"I can pull some strings. Slow roll the listing. You got

some money I can throw at the broker and owner? It'll help."

Greg nodded. "I got some."

His mother covered her ears. "I didn't hear that."

Henry laughed, then slapped his back. "I'll do what I can, but you gotta do your thing, son. Get your money and your people. We can't hold it off the market for long."

Greg rubbed his hands together, ready to put them back to work. Ready to build something new, to take another shot at his dream, and to get back the man he needed to help make it happen.

Chapter Four

"Yo, Anthony!"

"Yo, Tina!" Tony hollered back from behind the bar where he was slicing limes for the garnish caddy. "It's Tony, for the umpteenth time."

"Good luck with that," Sully said as he dumped a bowl of pitted cherries into one of the caddy compartments. "Twenty years together and she still calls me Sullivan. But if I dare call her Valentina..."

The leggy brunette strutted out from the pub's kitchen, her dark curls wobbling in a messy bun atop her head, a brightly patterned maxi dress flowing under her open chef's coat. "I heard that, mi amor," she said to her husband. She lifted the bar flip and joined them behind the bar. Stopping on the other side of Tony, she held her phone out to him. "I think this ad is about you, Anthony."

"Ad?"

"Yeah, I was posting in the classifieds section of an LGBTQ meetup app, trying to find this sexy blonde spitfire Sullivan and I hooked up with last month. All blonde hair, blue eyes, and black leather." She hummed her appreciation, while Sully blushed. "Anywho, I found this instead." She brandished her phone at him again, smiling. "Just read it, hermano."

He washed and dried his hands, then took the device and began to read aloud. "Dear Mr. Manhattan." A wide grin stretched across his face, making further words difficult.

"Well, well, well," Tina said, each word punctuated by a tap of her high heel. "Would you look at that? Someone's smitten."

So smitten that Tony hadn't slept with another man in nine months. He'd had to force himself to leave New Orleans that morning—the place and the man. He'd wanted nothing more than to stay wrapped in the chef's big arms, to kiss him good morning, and to run his hands over all that beautiful brown skin, his tongue over the ink he'd discovered on both shoulders. To see his deep dark eyes in the light of dawn and feel what the morning wood he'd been sporting could do. But if he'd stayed long enough to do any of those things, Tony would have never left. He had left, and he didn't regret that night or leaving, but he was certain no one would live up to such an incredible lay, so he hadn't bothered trying, even here in San Francisco, one of the most queer-friendly cities in the world.

Tina smacked her nicotine gum, snapping Tony back to the present. His eyes cut to her, more harshly than he'd intended, and he opened his mouth to apologize.

She raised a hand, cutting him off, and spat the gum

out in the under-bar trashcan in the most unladylike way possible. Tony loved her all the more for it. "My bad," she said. "Now, read us the rest."

"We met nine months ago at a bar in New Orleans," he resumed. "You were the too cute hipster behind the bar. I was the out-of-work chef acting the Virgin Mary with my too big hands." Hands that had been deliciously rough as they'd expertly teased Tony, opened him up, and stroked him to climax. He read on before he embarrassed himself. "You blew my mind with your cocktails, then you rocked my world and started it spinning again. I've got a gig for you. Dram, Bywater, New Orleans. Come drink with me. Yours, Mr. New Orleans."

"Yours?" Sully said, brow raised. "Who was he?"

Tony's cheeks heated to burning. "I didn't get his name. He was a chef who came into the bar I worked at in NOLA."

"What'd he cook?" Tina asked, always curious, always interested and eager to learn.

"I don't know." Three flops he'd said. "I think his restaurant had just closed."

"Sounds like he's got a new one. Maybe he wants you to work with him."

He handed the phone back to Tina. "He was a good fuck. That was all."

"This"—she brandished the device again—"is more than just a good fuck."

Sully passed him a handful of lemons. "You gonna go?"

"It was one night." He picked up his knife and began

quartering the fruit. "I'm not gonna uproot my life for a stranger."

"A stranger who is actively searching for you," Tina said.

"We can have our favorite feds check him out," Sully added, "if you're concerned."

Tony shook his head. "Nah, he was a good guy." He laid down the knife again and split a glance between the best bosses he'd ever worked for. "I can't just leave you guys in the lurch."

"Please." Tina flicked a hand toward the front doors. "This is San Francisco. I can spit and hit a bartender. I can replace you today."

He rolled his eyes. "Gee, thanks."

"Love you, baby." She presented her upturned cheek, which he dutifully pecked. She turned serious and a little sad, though, as she righted her gaze. "How much longer were you here for anyway?"

He pulled her into a hug. "This is the longest I've stayed anywhere in five years. And I never go back to the same place."

Sully laid a hand on his shoulder. "Some things, some people, are worth a return visit."

"Exactly." Tina drew back, smiling. She framed his face with her hands and patted his cheeks. "Just a visit. You don't have to stay there forever."

Except Tony feared if he got another taste of Mr. New Orleans, that's exactly what he'd want to do. Stay. Forever.

Tony drew back the gauzy curtain and stared out the motel room window, past the interstate, to the barren landscape dotted with oil rigs, all of it shimmering with heat. Texas in late April, at dusk, and it was ninety degrees outside. Eighty in here, if he had to guess. He fiddled with the dials on the ancient AC unit, turning it up to high.

It would have been cooler in the car, but not if he got stuck on the freeway in rush-hour traffic. So he'd stopped for the night at a motel on the western edge of Houston. Better than overheating the car and better than losing hours to traffic. This way he'd arrive in New Orleans midday tomorrow, at a decent hour, rather than God only knew when later tonight.

Those were the excuses he told himself.

His gaze glided back to the interstate, toward the city immediately ahead and to the one that lay six hours beyond. His thoughts drifted the same direction, to the gig and the man waiting for him in New Orleans. He could still reverse course to the West Coast or divert to Galveston or drive past the Big Easy to Pensacola, neither a town he'd visited yet. He could keep the promise he'd made to himself five years ago. A promise he hadn't once questioned until now. For a man he hardly knew. He turned from the window, snatched his keys off the dresser, and grabbed his suitcase. Galveston was looking better and better. He could head down there tonight. Be there in an hour.

He paused with his hand on the door.

Or he could sleep on it and decide in the morning when he wasn't worn out from driving three days straight.

"Fuck!" He spun on his heel, dropped his luggage, and tossed his keys onto the dresser again. "What are you going to do, Monaco?"

As if in answer, his phone rang, his sister's Springsteen ringtone competing with the droning AC. He crossed the room and flipped it down a notch, muting the racket. "Hey, Jules."

"Hey yourself. You make it there yet?"

"Not quite." He glanced back out the window. "Stopped before Houston. It's hot as balls, and I needed a rest."

"I don't doubt the first, but the second part of your statement is bullshit."

"Love you too," he managed around a laugh.

His four-year-old niece giggled in the background. "You said a bad word, Mommy," she chided her mother.

To which Julia mumbled, "Shit."

Elle giggled and clapped louder. "Again."

His sister groaned. "Mother of the year, right here."

"Don't be so hard on yourself," Tony said. "She's growing up in Queens. Not the first or last time she'll hear that word."

"This is true."

"Everything good there?" he asked.

"We're fine. And you will be too."

He plopped onto the end of the bed, billowing his shirt for breeze as the temperature climbed. "But I don't go—"

"Back to places, I know. And I know why. But were you going to do that forever? Like, even when you were seventy and a crotchety old New Yorker?"

He couldn't help but laugh, remembering their crotchety older relatives in their golden years. Brows bushier, tempers shorter, accents longer.

"That'd be impossible, Tony," his sister said, bringing him back to the present. "You were bound to return someplace sometime. Maybe you'll even come back here at some point. See the life Jake and I have built."

He flattened his hand against his chest, against the sudden throbbing behind his breastbone. "Jules, I'm so—"

"I said at some point, when you're ready. Until then, we'll come to you, wherever you're at. Jake and Elle like the adventure."

"Your family shouldn't—"

"*Our* family," she said. "And *you* shouldn't have had to spend all those years at home with Dad while I was at Syracuse. I got my degree, met Jake there, and now we have Elle and a home. You made this life possible. Coming to you, until you're ready to come to us, is the least we can do. Now, that's enough about the past." She huffed—end of discussion—and he could see his sister cocking her hip and swiping her dark curls away from her face. Elle was likely mimicking her. They were two women he was not about to argue with. On to their next mission. Him. "What are we going to do about your future?"

"I could just stay here. Or go to Galveston."

"You want me to scroll up and read you the texts from

the last time you tried Texas. Five days, Tony. You lasted five days."

He groaned and fell back onto the bed. She was right. Nothing against the Lone Star State, but it wasn't for him. Not enough places for him on the coast, and the hip factor of Austin wasn't enough to outweigh the landlocked claustrophobia.

"This gig in New Orleans…" Jules said, "It's a good opportunity for your career?"

Tony smiled and some of the weight lifted off his chest. He loved that his sister, a successful New York lawyer, like their dad had been before his accident, never once cast judgment on his profession. She demanded copies of his bar menus, tried his recipes at home, and was always sending him articles about opportunities and advancements in mixology. She wanted him to succeed and, like a dutiful older sibling, looked out for him.

"Maybe?" he replied. "I haven't talked to him yet. Maybe he wants me to design the beverage menu from scratch, or maybe he just wants me to work the late shift."

"There are plenty of bartenders in New Orleans. He wouldn't run a bunch of ads looking for you if he didn't want more." She'd checked; the ad Tina had found wasn't the only one. "He recognized your talent."

He tried and failed to muffle the strangled noise that escaped his lips, recalling the mutual "talents" he and Mr. New Orleans had shared.

"Okay, *talents*," Julia teased, accurately interpreting his dying-goose noises.

"Jesus." He covered his face with his hand and

doubted the heat he felt there had anything to do with the Texas temps.

But when Jules spoke again, the teasing tone was gone, replaced with warm sincerity. "Do you want to go, Anthony?"

He didn't question the immediacy of his answer, the answer right there on the tip of his tongue. He didn't question the truth of it either. He'd never lied to his sister, and today was no exception. "Yes."

Chapter Five

Greg hammered the last nail into Dram's new bar and mentally cheered. Not a single broken or bruised finger. When he'd first returned to New Orleans, he could barely hit the head of a nail; his left hand had been nothing but bruises. He was surprised his father—a contractor turned developer—hadn't disowned him. But like he'd told Manhattan, he'd learned to be a carpenter. Building shelters with his father's team and building three restaurants. Now on restaurant number four, he was confident enough with a hammer, saw, and blueprints to install his own custom bar—the centerpiece of his new concept. This was gonna be the one. He was even more sure of it today than he had been that day last summer when his parents had shown him the space. Even more sure than the morning he'd woken up alone, inspired yet missing the source of his inspiration.

"Stop mooning," a southern-tinged voice yelled over

the whir of the floor sander. The machine quieted a moment later, and a plaid bandana slapped Greg in the face a moment after that. "And wipe off before you drip sweat all over the place."

Greg wasn't a small guy by any stretch of the imagination, but the man lumbering his way, Michelin-starred chef Miller Sykes, was a mountain by comparison. The layer of sawdust powdering his chestnut beard, his cutoff denim shorts, and the sweat-stained plaid and gray tee he wore only enhanced the mountain-man image. Which was so far from the truth when it came to his marshmallow of a best friend that Greg laughed out loud.

"Floors done?" he asked, once he got his hilarity under control.

Miller gestured toward the dining area. Tables and chairs were a week out still, but it was starting to look real. Feel real. "Gotta sweep this dust out and sand around the bar after we edge it," Miller said. "But it should be ready for varnish Monday."

Nodding, Greg circled the bar through his now functioning bar flip and grabbed two bottles of Gravity Alto Pils out of the mini fridge. He popped the caps and passed one to Miller.

They tapped the bottle necks, then each downed half in one go. Good stuff. Miller's next words, however, were not so good. "We gonna talk about the glaring problem?"

Greg surveyed the fully assembled backbar, walked to the bar flip at the end, tested it, then passed under it and inspected the bar from the front as well. He spread his arms out wide. "What the fuck? I thought I was done."

"Building it, yeah." Miller sank onto the front bay window seat where a six-top table would eventually be situated. Miller, though, wasn't letting him enjoy that victory. "But you're six weeks from opening, and you haven't ordered any of the booze to fill it or put together a bar menu."

"I'll get to it."

"Babe, the name of the restaurant is Dram."

Greg flipped him the bird. "Next week, I swear, when they're doing the floors and I can't do anything else."

Miller's grin was knowing and devious. "You're still waiting."

Greg sat next to him and guzzled what was left of his Pilsner.

"How long ago did you post the ad?" Miller asked.

"Sometime after you gave me the tip about it at Christmas."

Miller nudged his shin. "Valteau…"

"Fine," Greg groaned. "The very next morning."

Miller laughed. "You're such a dork."

It both sucked and rocked having a friend who knew him so well.

Miller finished his beer and stood, snagging the empty from Greg's hands. "You can't keep waiting, babe. You need to hire a beverage director."

Greg fell sideways onto the bench seat, then rolled onto his back, staring up at the exposed wood ceiling beams and looking back into his mind for the mental picture of the dark haired, amber-eyed hipster writhing under him in bed. "He was perfect, Miller."

Glass bottles clanked, then heavy footsteps headed back his direction. "Because he poured a perfect cocktail or because he perfectly rode your dick?"

"Both," Greg admitted as he closed his eyes. "Is that a bad thing?"

"If it's making you stupid, yes." A shadow fell over him, and Miller's hip nudged him to the side, making room next to him. "You're up against the clock, and you've put so much work into this place. I can feel it." He laid a hand on Greg's chest, over his heart. "You can too."

Yeah, he could. Greg covered Miller's hand with his and squeezed. "I think this is the one."

He'd woken up that morning nine months ago in Manhattan's bed, had a self-pitying shot of sublime barrel-aged cocktail, and the notion at the back of his mind had first started to take shape. A concept, a name. It had gotten stronger when he'd first seen this place, stronger still when he'd peeled back the brown paper that covered most of the stained-glass transom above the door. Inlaid in copper was the word *Haven*. Perfect for the community gathering space he envisioned. He'd had a business partner by Thanksgiving, multiple investors by Christmas, permits by the end of January. And now here he was in late April, down to the finishing touches. The pieces—all but one—had fallen into place. The fourth time was gonna be the charm. But Miller was right. He couldn't wait much longer for the final missing piece. He'd have to move on without it and hope its absence didn't spoil the dream.

"I'll give him through the weekend."

Miller's hand squeezed around his. "Don't think you'll need that long."

Greg startled, a zing of hope racing up his spine. He turned his head and opened his eyes to look past Miller... and saw the one.

Manhattan stood in the doorway, looking every bit as delicious as Greg remembered—tight cargo shorts, fitted T-shirt, a linen scarf draped around his neck, and his Mohawk of black curls moussed high.

Miller momentarily blocked his view, bending to whisper in his ear, "I take back everything I said. He's fucking perfect."

"And mine," Greg practically growled.

Miller chuckled as he released his hand and stood. "Then go get him."

The big man winked as he strode past Tony, and Tony would be lying if he said he didn't sneak a peek at his ass in those denim shorts. He turned back to Greg Valteau—Tony had googled the highly-anticipated Dram and read up on its owner—who Tony was pleased to see was still checking out his body instead. "Boyfriend?" he asked.

"Best friend."

Tony shouldn't care, not if he was here in a strictly professional capacity for the gig the ad mentioned. But still, he was glad he didn't have to compete with a giant like that—whose size and presence effortlessly filled the room—in any manner.

"Restaurant number four?" he said.

Greg righted himself and spread his arms. "What can I say? I'm a junkie."

"It's a gorgeous space." Tony strolled to the bar and ran his hand across the top. It needed a coat of lacquer, but the smooth wood grain was irregular and unique. "This is gorgeous too."

"Except it's incomplete." Greg was suddenly right behind him, and Tony sucked in a breath. "You're not standing behind it."

"The gig your ad mentioned…"

"I need a beverage director."

Tony moved to turn, but Greg laid a hand on his hip, fingers spread. Tony closed his eyes and struggled to breathe, the memories of their night together rushing back to drown him. He loved the weight of Greg's big hand on him. Could only imagine how rough it would feel after building another bar.

"Hear me out." Greg rotated him, then stepped back, and Tony could breathe again. Until Greg added, "We open in six weeks."

"Six weeks?" he squawked. "And you don't have—"

Greg pressed a finger to his lips. "I already heard it from the grumpy bear." He dropped his finger before Tony was tempted to suck it into his mouth. "I was waiting for you."

"Why me?"

"Because you inspired this place."

"Me?" Fuck, why was he so fucking squeaky?

Greg smiled, sexy as all get out. "It's called Dram, Mr. Manhattan."

Tony returned the infectious grin. "So you're just going to serve Manhattans?"

"I wish I could get away with that, but no." Greg stepped away, around and behind the bar, across from Tony. "But I do want the bar, the drinks, the crowd it draws, and the community it builds and supports to be the stars here, the centerpieces. My previous ventures, I was too focused on the food. Hyperlocal, then hyper fancy, then fucking all over the place with no cohesive vision." He spread his hands over the bar top. "This will bring it all together."

"No offense," Tony said, palms raised before laying them on the bar. "But how is that different than half the other places in this town?"

"One, because I want it to be a safe space for NOLA's queer community. And two, because I'll have you." Greg winked. "And you're the best."

The compliment felt good, tempting, on top of the chance to do something for his career and his community, and to do it with the handsome temptation grinning across the bar from him. "Listen, Greg—"

"Hey!" Greg's brown eyes widened, the corner crinkles smushing a freckle by the right one. "You know my name, but I don't know yours."

Tony extended a hand to him. "Anthony Monaco. I go by Tony."

Greg shook his hand... and didn't let go. "Help me launch this, Tony, and I'll make it worth your while."

Already worth it for the chance to stare into those deep, earnest brown eyes again. Dangerous too. Even knowing that, Tony wasn't about to turn down the offer. As scary as it was, it was also too good on too many fronts to pass up. Provided Greg could do one thing for him... "Just one request. I need to know upfront or me working here, with you, won't work."

Greg's smile faltered, and his shoulders tensed, like he was preparing for the last thing he wanted to hear. "What's that?"

Nothing so dire. "I need music or some other noise any time we're eating or trying food. I can't handle the sound of a person chewing in the quiet. Even someone smacking gum is like nails on a chalkboard for me."

Greg's smile returned, bigger, like he'd solved a mystery and won a prize. "That's why you work in bars?"

Tony nodded. "Drowns it all out."

"We're already wired for sound." He pointed out several speakers, each discreetly tucked between jutting bricks in the walls. "All set there."

"One other thing," Tony said before he lost his will to say what he needed. "We should keep this professional."

"If that's what you want."

"It's not what I want," Tony confessed. "But it's what I need if I'm going to leave here after the launch."

He thought Greg's smile would falter again. That that was what he hadn't wanted to hear earlier. Instead, Greg's gorgeous grin turned wicked and impossibly more handsome as he braced his forearms on the bar and leaned across it. "I'll promise you this," he said, voice low and vibrating with temptation. Knees weak, Tony gave more of his weight to the bar, which brought them closer. Close enough he could feel the heat of Greg's breath when he uttered the promise that would seal Tony's fate. "I promise I won't make the first move."

Chapter Six

Tony arrived outside the front door of Dram... and cringed. The racket inside did not sound good. Greg had said the floors were being varnished this week, but whatever was going on inside sounded like demo, not like staining the floors. What had happened in the day and a half since he'd last seen Greg? They'd chatted—flirted—some more that day, then Tony had left to find a rental while Greg spent time with Miller before he left town. Greg had offered Tony his guest room upstairs, but that was way too much temptation. Thankfully, his old rental was vacant again and not too far away, which was why he was early for their ten o'clock. He raised his fist to knock.

"Don't bother." Greg rounded the corner of the building, striding toward him in jeans and a faded LSU tee. "Can't hear shit."

"What's going on in there?"

"Just leveling some things before they start with the varnish." The *smash* and *bang* from the other side of the door sounded far more serious than 'just leveling,' but Greg didn't give him time to question. He was a man in motion, shoving a handful of canvas bags into Tony's hands, then walking on past him down the street. "We've got other work to do."

Tony caught up with him a half block later. "Like shopping?"

"Farmer's market."

"A little late, isn't it? I thought you chefs were first in line."

Greg grinned. "We won't be serving brunch at Dram, and not only because hollandaise is the devil."

"You mean angel, right? All that buttery goodness."

"Fuck you. Not in my kitchen."

Tony laughed out loud, and Greg shot him the bird. The gesture, however, was belied by the chef's teasing smile. Tony pretended not to feel it in his dick.

"I'm also shit at the morning thing," Greg said as they made their way toward the water. "Which is why I treat the purveyors well. They hold what I need until I make it there. Or if I'm feeling adventurous, I send my sous out to shop." He nodded toward the bags in Tony's hand. "Which is how we're going to play this today."

Tony froze midstep across the street from the park where multi-colored umbrellas dotted the pathway. "You want me to shop? But I'm not a chef."

"You are. The most important chef in this venture. I may have mentioned the Balcones Bomb when I pitched Dram to my business partner and our investors."

Pressure cemented Tony's feet to the sidewalk. He

hadn't thought this through enough. What if falling for the sexy chef wasn't the biggest risk? Said sexy chef was risking it all—on him and his talents behind the bar. It was an amazing opportunity—once in a lifetime, perhaps—but anyone could see how much Dram meant to Greg. What if he didn't live up to the hype Greg had built up in his mind? What if he cratered this venture not because he had a soft spot for his boss but because he wasn't good enough? "Greg, I—"

"Breathe, Manhattan."

The nickname calmed him, as did Greg's hand on his shoulder, squeezing it gently. He directed them across the street, and they fell into step with the crowd. "I'm sorry, I come on strong, I know."

"You don't say?"

They reached the edge of the market setup, and Greg drew them off the path, out of the way of passersby. His ever-present smile was infused with the sun and an even deeper warmth that promised addiction. "I need your help, Tony." As did his earnest words in that New Orleans drawl. "I meant what I said the other day. I want the bar, the gathering place for our community, to be at the center of the Dram concept. We'll work out the details of that together, one day, one step at a time. Today is just the first of those. Let's see how we work together." Greg smirked. "Besides in bed."

Tony laughed, the professional pressure vanishing, as he returned to worrying about the problem in his pants and the handsome man his dick wanted to chase after.

They rejoined the moving mass of people, strolling

amid the tables of bright and fresh delights. Tony gravitated toward the vendor selling fresh flowers, the stems of lavender catching his eye, sparking an idea, as did several of the other blooms and herbs. Garnishes and subtle flavorings he could work with. He purchased a sampling, and without missing a beat, Greg next directed them to a fruit vendor where Tony gathered a variety of citrus items. Lemons, yuzu, white grapefruit—late winter and early spring varieties.

"All right," Greg said, after another minute of Tony coveting a crate of blood oranges. "You finish up here. I know what I need to do." He handed his credit card to the woman behind the register. "Cass, take care of him. And we'll take the full crate."

"Just like that? You don't even know what I'm going to make."

"I got the gist." He moved on, calling out a greeting in French to the greens purveyor a few tables over.

"You know he's one of the best chefs in the city, right?"

Tony rotated back to the raven-haired woman behind the register. "I haven't gotten the chance to eat at one of his places yet," he told her.

"Divine." She blew a chef's kiss as she weighed out the produce in his bag. "This a sign of what's to come?"

"I hope so." He extended a hand. "Tony Monaco. I'm working with Greg on the beverage menu."

"Excellent. Cassandra Talbott," she said, returning the greeting. "We'll be talking again, I'm sure. I source most of Greg's fruit, and the wife and I have been watching Dram come along. We can't wait."

A little of the pressure returned, but in a good way. "We can't wait to have you."

By the time they finished at the farmer's market, then swung by the store where Greg admired Tony's quick and efficient shopping for the liquor and mixers he needed, then by the butcher shop where Greg was much less efficient, and finally by Port of Call for burgers to-go, it was midafternoon when they returned to a much quieter Dram.

Well, mostly quiet.

"Gregory, mijo, come see!"

"Agree with whatever she says," he told Tony as they dropped their bags in the kitchen. His father had given him the same advice many moons ago, and where the spitfire standing at the edge of the dining room was concerned, it was gospel.

And his general contractor had delivered one hell of a miracle today. "You do good work, Gloria."

"Of course I do," she preened, but the blush on her cheeks conveyed her appreciation of the compliment, which was more than due. She'd saved his ass.

This morning, he had come downstairs to find water standing in one corner of the dining area. He'd feared the entire floor would need to be replaced, no small feat given the reclaimed wood they'd sourced. And no small feat given the custom furniture arriving next week and the staff arriving the week after. If he had to delay, he risked his chefs and servers finding other jobs, risked his soft opening date for the critics, risked his grand opening in time for Pride.

He hadn't let on about any of that to Tony. The last thing he needed was to spook his beverage director on day one. Greg had called Gloria, and she'd taken charge, rolling up her shirts sleeves and assuring him she'd handle it. Which she'd done, marvelously. The replaced floor boards were a perfect match, the varnish on the entire floors nicely complemented the bar, and the brown paper over the door had been removed, allowing sunlight to stream in through the freshly cleaned stained glass, casting a rainbow of light across the shining floors and bar.

Tony gasped behind him. "Holy shit. I didn't think it could get more beautiful in here, but it's…"

Greg glanced over his shoulder. "Perfect." Their gazes met and held, the same splash of color reflected in Tony's golden irises. Greg would have broken his no-first-move promise if not for Gloria clearing her throat.

"Manners, mijo," she teased.

Chuckling, he shifted a step so he could introduce the woman who'd helped make all this possible. "Tony Monaco, meet Gloria Ramos, best general contractor in the city. And all those silver curls"—he gestured at the pile of gray curls on top of Gloria's head—"are my fault."

"Esa es la verdad!" She moved past him with a playful shove. "I should warn you this one's middle name is trouble."

Tony laughed. "I got that same warning from half a dozen vendors today. Seems to be a trend." He rested the orange crate on his hip and extended his hand. "Encantado de conocerla, Gloria."

Greg smiled. He'd overheard Tony conversing in Spanish with several vendors today. No doubt he'd been following his and Gloria's byplay. "Tony's my new beverage director."

"You make *some* good choices." She shot him a wink, then returned her attention to Tony. "Welcome aboard."

Greg headed for the kitchen while Tony and Gloria continued to converse in Spanish behind him, Gloria explaining how she'd met Greg's family in Houston, post-Katrina, volunteering at a shelter. They got to talking, Henry learned what she did for a living, and he enticed her to New Orleans with the GC title, a glass ceiling she hadn't been able to break in Houston. She had shattered it here as the foreperson on his dad's biggest projects, on the shelters his parents' nonprofit had built, and on Greg's restaurants. And with each restaurant build, she'd patiently let him help, taught him all the basics he lacked, and rescued his ass as needed, like today.

Entering the kitchen, she circled the island and peeked into their bags. "What are you cooking?"

"I haven't told him yet," Greg replied as he flipped on some music using the app on his phone.

"And I haven't told him what I'm mixing," Tony added.

Gloria cackled. "Oh, he's a keeper."

"No argument here," Greg replied. She laughed some more as she headed for the exit, until Greg called after her.

He waited for her to turn, then pressed his palms together over his chest. "Thank you for today, truly."

"Of course, mijo." She graced him with a kind departing smile, gave Tony one too, then disappeared out the back.

"You want to tell me what that was about?" Tony asked as he unloaded bags.

"Overnight leak." Greg fetched two water bottles from the fridge and set them next to the to-go boxes on the pass. "I was worried about the floors."

"That's what all the banging was about this morning?"

Greg cast his gaze aside and pushed food and water toward Tony. "Didn't want to spook you."

Tony's fingers closed around his wrist. "That's not what's going to spook me, New Orleans." His fingers ghosted across the inside of Greg's wrist, and Greg nearly broke his promise again. Tony released him before he could pounce. "You don't have to carry that shit alone. We're partners in this, yeah?"

Greg gulped down his glee at hearing Tony's words and wrangled his emotions into a nod. Then drowned them in meat and cheese. Tony seemed to do the same, attacking his burger with gusto. He let loose a pleasure-laced moan that had Greg rounding the island, needing to hide his body's reaction. Fucking hell, what was he thinking? How was he supposed to keep this professional? He more than respected Manhattan's professional prowess, but all that competency, watching him work today, *was* seduction in and of itself.

Greg took another bite of burger. Focus on the food, he

coached himself. Not the handsome hipster an arm's length away with grease running down his chin, over fingers he'd like to— *Fuck!* He needed to cook, needed to distract his mind and his hands before they reached out and grabbed what he wanted.

He made quick work of the rest of his burger, washed his hands, and grabbed his chef's coat off the wall peg. He snagged the apron beside it and tossed it to Tony. "You might have to size this down a bit. Dad is even bigger than I am."

"Cooking family, then?"

"Everyone but my mom." He shrugged into his coat and rolled up his sleeves. "She says she thanks God daily for blessing her with a husband and son who can cook."

Tony laughed all the way to the sink.

Greg dumped their boxes and made space for them to work. "How long do you need for the first drink?"

"Five minutes or so," Tony said as he donned the apron. "I think this one will be quick."

"Okay, I'll follow your lead and do something quick as well."

Five minutes later, Greg was sipping a divine twist on the French 75, while enjoying endive leaves stuffed with duck rillettes and topped with a drizzle of honey.

"This is amazing," Tony said around a bite.

"As is your drink."

"I saw the lavender this morning, and it reminded me of all the purple and yellow around here." He flicked his fingers at Greg's LSU tee. "I wanted to riff on that."

"It's the right vibe to go with something like this." He

lifted another duck-filled leaf. "Simple, yet elevated. A twist on a classic and a tribute to local ingredients. What are we calling it?"

Tony licked the honey off his fingers, and Greg had to force himself to concentrate on the hipster's words. "Twisted French?"

"Uh-huh." Greg finished his last bite and returned the torture, pleased and amused by Tony's strangled noise and quick redirect toward the crate of oranges. Greg was rubbing his hands together when Tony turned back around, and that only made Manhattan blush harder. Maybe Greg wasn't the only one operating with a semi. He gave them both an out, equally encouraged by their culinary progress. "What's next?"

"This one might take a little longer," Tony said. "I'm still working it out."

"Sounds good. I've got a couple things I want to get started, a few sauces for you to taste that I'll use on pork. A Drambuie glaze for ribs and a mojo for pork shoulder. I think they'll go well with the flavors you bought."

Tony paused and the look of wonder he gave Greg was downright intoxicating. "The *flavors* I bought. Not the food."

Greg snatched an orange from the crate and tossed it in the air. "I see the fruit first, of course. It's the word association we're taught first. But a split second later, I think about the flavors, which is the association I obsess over. Take this guy." He tossed it in the air again. "Tart, citrusy, but with an undercurrent of sweetness, a berry flavor almost, that other varieties of oranges lack. From there I think about what will balance that out or what will bring out more of the unique flavors."

Tony was smiling and nodding. "That's why I picked up the elderflower. Add the prosecco for a spritz, maybe also one of the more herbal gins to round out the sweetness but keep it fresh."

"I can also use the fruit for a vinaigrette. Pair it with bitter lettuces and a pungent cheese to balance out the dressing and the drink."

Tony's smile widened. "Fuck yeah. This is totally gonna work."

Better than they both anticipated, if Greg had to bet.

"This isn't what I ordered!" Greg's voice reached Tony's ears over the whirring fan of the temperature-controlled wine closet and over the sultry notes of Adele filling the pub. "You sent me glass shelves. I ordered hammered copper!"

In the two weeks they'd worked together, Greg frequently got loud, but it was always with excitement. Boisterous was an apt adjective for the big man. Before today, Tony had never heard Greg's voice raised in anger, his drawl brimming over with frustration and disap-pointment.

He settled the last bottle of Grenache in its wooden cubby, stepped around the case boxes littering the floor, and popped into the dining room to see what was going on.

Greg stood behind the bar, glaring at two cardboard

boxes lying open on the bar top. "I've got custom gaps in my mirrored backbar wall where copper plates and shelves are supposed to go." As if the person on the phone could see him, Greg lifted out an L-shaped piece of glass, rotated it, and held it up to one of the gaps. "These are glass, and they don't fucking fit. Where are my shelves?"

He was right; there were four to six inches of wall showing below the glass L-shelf, right where the wider copper plate and shelf should have fit instead. The large backbar mirror and backing brace had been custom designed and cut with beveled openings for the staggered shelves, which would hold different types of liquor. Hammered copper shelves, which had been custom ordered to match the copper *Haven* etched in the stained-glass transom above the front door.

Tony glanced back and forth between the two—the gaps in the wall and the stained-glass window—racking his brain for a solution... and finding it in the kaleidoscope of light cast by the transom. It could work. In fact, it could amplify the haven message he and Greg wanted to project for Dram, maybe even better than the original design.

"Portland! What the fuck are they doing in Portland?" Greg's knuckles blanched around the edge of the glass shelf he held. "When can you get them here?"

Expecting the worst, Tony hustled behind the bar and laid a hand on Greg's back, making his presence known. With the other, he tugged the glass shelf out of Greg's hand.

Just in time.

"Eight weeks?" Greg shouted. An angry blush streaked

across his cheekbones all the way up to the tips of his ears. "I can't wait eight weeks. I open in four... No, don't put me on ho—Fuck!"

Tony carefully laid the shelf back in the box—they'd need it; they'd need all of them—and skirted under Greg's raised arm, around to his front. "Hang up the phone, New Orleans."

Greg stared at him like he'd just suggested pairing Cabernet with caviar. "I waited fifteen minutes to talk to a human. I can't hang up now."

"Hang. Up." Tony grasped his bulging biceps and tugged it down, pulling the phone away from his ear. "I've got an idea. I think we can make it work."

Frustration bled into panic as Greg waved a hand at the boxes of glass. "But this isn't the design. Those pieces don't fit."

"You're right, they don't." Tony placed his hands on Greg's chest, aiming to calm him. Distract him, if nothing else. Never mind how solid, how warm the hard muscles were beneath the chef's threadbare tee. Never mind how much Tony would like to see and taste that chest again, run his tongue over darkened nipples and faded ink, bury his nose in the crease between thigh and groin and smell—Greg's sharp inhale yanked Tony out of the fantasy, out of the chaos heating his own blood and back to the chaos that needed avoiding here. "I can make them work," Tony said. "Maybe even better than the copper. Do you trust me?"

Dark, anxious eyes stared down at him, a plea in them that Tony was desperate to answer. More than anything, he wanted to help this kind, talented man make his dream come true. A dream that was also becoming his own. Tony swallowed down that fearful thought and held Greg's gaze.

A giant breath later, Greg ended the call and tossed the phone between the boxes on the bar. "I trust you." He covered Tony's hands, holding them against his chest, and lowered his forehead to rest against Tony's. "I just wasn't expecting the eleventh-hour setback."

"It's a restaurant opening. Where have you been?"

Greg chuckled. "I know. We'll probably have another hiccup or twenty before eleven fifty-nine. I just want this to be perfect."

Tony drew back before the warm breath skirting over his lips tempted him closer. "I know you do. So do I." Greg's hopeful, trusting gaze tempted him still, almost enough for Tony to make the first move, but he stopped himself. Barely. One hurdle at a time. He took another step back but left a hand in Greg's, tugging him away from the near-disaster and out from behind the bar. "I can fix this if you'll come with me."

Greg's roughly uttered "Anywhere" was the most tempting torture of all.

Chapter Seven

Greg was seriously regretting his promise to not make the first move. To not reach out and touch, to not taste, to not bend Tony over the bar and take him with his cock that had been half-hard every day since Tony had walked through the damn door.

Every day working together had been heaven and hell. Close quarters in which to watch Tony's nimble fingers mix cocktails, his lean muscles bunch and stretch whenever he shook a drink, his brows furrow and long lashes lower as he concentrated on recipes. The thoroughness with which he walked the bar staff through his bible, the patience he exhibited when explaining the suggested pairings to the servers, and the care he showed to Greg's kitchen staff making sure they were always apprised to any changes and stocked with the non-alcoholic drinks they needed while working, only proved the kind of man Tony was, on top of all that talent and sexiness.

Absolute torture.

It wouldn't last long. A thought Greg kept reminding himself of because this—working with and being around Tony—felt more right every day. Especially as they neared Dram's opening and things kicked into high gear. One week until they ripped the brown paper off the front windows and soft opened for the critics. A week later, they would open to the general public.

"Hey, Earth to New Orleans."

"Oh, sorry." Greg snagged another bottle from the box —Craneo Mezcal—and passed it to Tony, who was halfway up the ladder stocking shelves. Eyes lifted, they drifted to Tony's ass in another pair of snug fitting cargo shorts.

"You're checking out my ass again."

"Do you have any idea how good it looks? And where the fuck did you find cargo shorts that tight? Kind of defeats their purpose."

Tony threw him a wink. "Depends on the purpose."

"Cheeky, Manhattan."

"Yes." He grinned and added an extra wiggle of his ass as he descended two ladder rungs. "Next bottle?" he said, hand outstretched. "Should just be the Appleton Joy left."

With a barely restrained growl, and the barely restrained desire to launch himself at the gorgeous asshole who'd become his friend and right hand, Greg handed him the squat bottle of aged rum. "Yep, that's the last one."

Tony scaled the ladder a final time, up to the top shelf where he placed the rum, then climbed down a step and leaned back, balancing on one foot. "Not too bad."

"Not too bad" was an understatement. The bar was everything Greg had wanted. From the hand-assembled bar, to the cocktail menu Tony expertly crafted, to this amazing display and the bottles in it. An understated and limited collection—spirits carefully chosen by Tony for their contents and bottles, works of art in and of themselves. And beneath each glass shelf, in that space that had nearly given Greg a heart attack, were mosaics of stained glass, the color denoting the spirit, and arranged across the wall to form the overall impression of a rainbow. It was subtle and understated, but a clear tie to the stained glass above the door, and as Tony had predicted, an amplification of their message. New Orleans's LGBTQ community was welcome here. A safe haven in which to gather, to celebrate momentous occasions, to meet the person of their dreams. Like Greg had nearly a year ago in a different bar. The man who'd come up with this idea and worked it so seamlessly into Greg's vision for Dram, bringing it all together, like Greg knew he would.

He laid a hand on Tony's calf. "It's gorgeous, baby."

Maybe not the best thing to do or say with Tony balanced on one foot, on a ladder. The bartender wobbled, foot slipping, arms flailing, and the next thing Greg knew, his arms were full of hipster. His nose full of the smell he hadn't been able to shake for months—bergamot soap, sweat, and charred whiskey barrels. He leaned forward to take a taste—Tony's neck was right there—but stopped himself just shy of lips hitting skin. "I'm sorry, I just..." He lifted his head and looked at the bar, rather than at the man whose face was achingly close to his. "It's perfect." Warm breath washed over Greg's temple, nimble fingers curled around either side of his neck, and Greg gave in a little, glancing back at Tony. His black curls were wild, his cheeks flushed, and his eyes were the color of the rum he'd just handled. "You're perfect."

Tony shifted in his arms, bowing his back and gliding his hands higher to cradle the back of Greg's head. Tony brought the corner of his mouth into teasing contact with Greg's. "Fucking hell, New Orleans, just kiss me already."

First move made, Greg was happy to make the next, sealing their mouths in a kiss that sent lightning spiraling through his body, the strikes brightest in his heart, gut, and dick. He wanted this perfect man more than he'd wanted anyone. Right here, right now.

Tony obliged, wrapping his arms around Greg's neck and rocking a thick erection against his middle. Greg grasped his ass harder, spreading his cheeks, and Tony groaned. Not missing an opportunity, Greg dove his tongue between Tony's parted lips, tasting and tangling, claiming what he could now that Tony was back in his arms.

Mouths still greedily devouring, Greg spun and set Tony on the bar top. Stepping between his dangling legs, Greg dragged his hands up Tony's thighs.

Tony broke the kiss on a gasped curse. "Fuck, I missed those hands."

Greg would have snuck them under Tony's shorts if they weren't so damn tight. But the snugness made the erection straining behind the zipper all the more impressive. Greg framed it with his hands, thumbs teasing the crease of Tony's balls and the length of his cock.

Keening, Tony braced his arms behind him and arched

his back, thrusting Greg's direction. Greg spread his legs farther, leaned down, and mouthed his cock through the material on either side of the zipper. "Still pissed I didn't get longer with you that night."

Tony's arms began to slip, his lower body writhing. "Please. Just fuck me. Now."

"You're not getting off that easy, Manhattan." Greg moved to Tony's fly, unbuttoning and unzipping, and nudged his shorts down enough to repeat his earlier motions over the fabric of Tony's briefs. It was his turn to tease, to tempt, to torture. He was gonna love every minute of it, and Tony would too. He nudged under Tony's cock, gave his balls an open-mouthed kiss through the cotton, and blew hot breath across his taint. "I'm gonna eat you out."

Tony shivered. "Fuck..."

Greg moved back up and nipped along Tony's cock. "Then I'm gonna suck your cock."

Whatever Tony mumble-groaned was unintelligible.

"And then I'm gonna fuck you." Greg grabbed the backs of Tony's knees, yanked him forward, and thrust his own hips up, his rock-hard cock notching against Tony's taint. "Right here on our bar."

Through the haze of lust, it took Greg a moment to realize Tony hadn't reacted the same way to that last promise as he had the others. The muscles under his hands were stiff, the groans and pleas had stopped, and when Greg looked up, Tony's gaze was cast aside, his face turned away, like he no longer wanted to witness these proceedings.

Greg instantly righted himself and stepped back. "Baby…"

As if the spell-turned-nightmare had been broken, Tony wrenched himself up and off the bar. Greg caught his wrist, stopping his retreat toward the exit. "I'm sorry," he said to Tony's back, the other man not turning around. "Whatever I said or did, I'm sorry. I shouldn't have—"

Tony shook his head. "No, I'm the one who's sorry." He turned, and the deep sorrow and sadness in his amber eyes made Greg stumble back a step, then forward two, wanting to comfort. Tony, however, held up a hand, and Greg halted. "You've been wonderful," Tony said. "Dram is going to be wonderful. But I think it's time for me to go."

Greg's insides twisted like a pretzel. "Please don't—"

Tony cut off his words with a kiss, gentle and fleeting. "I'm sorry, New Orleans. I can't do this. But you can. Number four is going to be the one."

Greg was still speechless, and freshly hopeless, as the door swung shut behind the man he no longer wanted to do this without. His one.

Chapter Eight

The phone rang, and Greg lunged, snatching it off the bar top and checking the caller ID. His heart fell. Not the call he wanted. Fast on the heels of disappointment careened guilt for ever dismissing a call from his best friend.

"Hey, buddy," he answered, feigning nonchalance.

Not well enough. "Uh-oh, what's wrong?" Miller asked.

He could lie, or he could tell the truth and talk this out with someone who knew the stakes, better than most. "Another fucking hiccup." Not quite eleven-fifty-nine but close enough." He ran a hand over his head as he wove through the pub tables. "I fucked up, Miller. This is going to fail."

"No, it's not. You always—"

"I lost my beverage director."

Greg couldn't help but laugh at the high-pitched "*What?*" that had no business coming out of a man as big as Miller.

"I pressed too hard and scared him off."

The pop and hiss of a beer cap was unmistakable. A gulp later, Miller had his voice back. "Okay, Valteau, start from the top."

He filled Miller in on everything he'd shared with Tony the past four weeks. The tastings, the menus, the laughs, the first hiccup, a picture of the wall with Tony's elegant solution.

"You haven't lost him," Miller said.

"He said it was time for him to go. He hasn't answered any of my calls. He—"

"One look at that wall, and I can tell you that bar means as much to him as it does to you. He gets it, and he gets you."

"What if that's not enough?"

"Babe, breathe." Miller waited for him to inhale twice. "Now go behind your bar and get a shot of whiskey."

Greg followed the advice and, after a shot of Four Roses, felt a measure calmer. "Better, thank you." He tossed back another, then set the glass in the bar sink. "What am I gonna do, Miller?"

"God help us, but you need to put on your Detective Valteau cap."

"Fuck you."

"Made you laugh though, didn't it?"

He had, the asshole. And Miller knew him well enough to keep playing into Greg's amateur detective streak. "Do you know why he reacted the way he did? And don't say it's because you pushed too hard. I saw the way he looked at you when I was there. This isn't one-sided. He wants you too."

Greg mentally rewound every conversation he'd had with Tony, from the past four weeks and from nine months ago. "Something happened, five or so years ago. He hasn't stopped moving since."

"Moving or running?" Miller asked, a heightened note of concern coloring his North Carolina drawl.

"Moving," Greg assured him. "I've never gotten the impression he's being chased. Just needs to keep moving. Like he doesn't want to be in one place for too long." Another flash of memory from last summer. "He said he doesn't visit the same place twice."

"But he came back for you and Dram. He's attached to you and that bar. That backbar wall proves it."

"It scares him," Greg put together. "That attachment." He leaned against the bar and laid a hand over his heart, futilely trying to soothe the pain there. Not for himself, but for Tony. "Fuck. I gotta find out why."

"Yeah, you do, and whether you can help him overcome it, because you two need each other."

And Dram needed them both.

Tony didn't go straight back to his rental. If this was his last day in New Orleans, he had several stops to make. Iced coffee from French Truck, beignets from Du Monde, another burger from Port of Call, a cherry hand pie. He savored each treat one last time, because this would be his last ever trip to the Big Easy. He would never be able to return here and not run straight into Gregory Valteau's arms.

The fears he'd had before leaving San Francisco, the ones he'd confessed to his sister on the road here, were one hundred percent founded. The pull to stay in New Orleans and with Greg at Dram—our bar, he'd called it, and that's what it felt like now—was so strong Tony almost went back on the promise he'd made to himself five years ago. He'd had to leave, had to get out of there before he was well and truly fucked in more ways than one. So he visited his favorite NOLA spots, tucked the cherished memories away next to his aching heart, and struggled to button it up. When he returned to his rental, he couldn't flop onto the mattress and cry. He needed to pack and get on the road. There were still hours of summer twilight left.

He rounded the corner onto his street, saw the man sitting on his front stoop, and mentally scrapped his head start out of town. This was the other reason he'd spent time out after fleeing the bar. He'd hoped Greg would've given up by now. The text messages had dwindled over the past hours, and he'd thought it safe to return. Stupid. Greg had instead gone to the place he knew Tony would have to return to eventually. The man had persevered in some of the toughest kitchens in New York and was on his fourth restaurant here. He didn't give up.

Tony ate the last bite of his pie and crinkled up the pouch. Greg lifted his head, eyes darting from his phone to Tony, then to the plastic wrapper in his hand. "You hang around a while longer, I'll get you the real thing, not that imitation version."

Tony halted in his tracks, and Greg lifted a hand. "Sorry, sorry. Hubig's versus Haydel's is a touchy subject for us locals."

"That's not why I stopped."

"I know. A man can dream." Greg tucked his phone into his pocket and glanced over his shoulder at the rental. "You liked this place enough to come back to it."

Tony forced his feet to move and forced his heart to slow and stop trying to beat out of his chest. "Timing worked out."

"Like it did for you to come back to New Orleans?"

"No," Tony admitted as he came to stand in front of Greg. "I made time for that."

Greg snagged one of his belt loops and tugged him closer. "Talk to me, Manhattan. If nothing else, I'd like to think we're friends now."

"We are." Tony couldn't resist running a hand over Greg's head, loving the way the short hairs tickled his fingertips. Loving the dark, earnest eyes that looked up at him with genuine concern. Loving... They were friends, and more, judging by the way all that love tugged at the center of his chest. Which was why he couldn't stay. The pull would only get stronger, and it would be even harder to leave when he had to.

He dropped a kiss on the crown of Greg's head, then sat on the stoop next to him. It was hot and humid tonight, so very unlike the West Coast, but it reminded Tony of home. Maybe that's also why the fear had kicked in so hard and fast today. But it was cooler now than it had been earlier, and people were out on the street, heading to dinner and enjoying the evening. Also like evenings in the City. That was as good a place as any to start his story. "I stayed still for a long time. In New York."

"Because of your dad?"

Of course Greg had caught that. And remembered it still, nine months later. Not only was he a great chef, he was also observant. Sometimes a little too much, but it was endearing. And it helped move this particular conversation along.

"My mom left when I was a kid, so it was just me, Dad, and my sister, Julia. He was a lawyer, and we lived well, relatively, for Manhattan. And then an accident happened my freshman year of high school. He was hit by a car on his way to work. Fucked up his spine, which led to a whole host of other health issues."

"The drinks you mentioned?"

"Helped with the pain. He tried to work through it, but that didn't last long. He wasn't a drunk or mean when he drank. Nothing like that. It just eased the pain, as much as anything could for someone in that much agony."

Greg threw an arm around him, and Tony accepted the offered comfort. "I stayed home," he continued. "And Jules went to college." When Greg tensed, Tony rushed to add, "I didn't begrudge her that in the least. I wasn't the best student, so college was never going to be for me."

Greg relaxed, even chuckled a little. "Same with Miller. He went straight into a kitchen. No college, no culinary school, and he's the best chef I know."

"Kind of the same here. I took online bartending cour-ses, tested out recipes with my dad, and once I turned twenty-one, on the one weekend a month my sister visited, I'd work nonstop at one of the bars in the Village that needed extra weekend hands. Two years doing that."

"Worked up a good savings?" At Tony's nod, Greg added, "But you eventually left?"

"Dad passed away five years ago. I left the day after his funeral."

Greg released a giant breath and held Tony tighter. "And you never stopped moving."

He buried his nose in Greg's shoulder. "I loved my dad, he was my hero, but being stuck in that house..." He swallowed hard, remembering the feeling of the walls closing in, of the sound of his father chewing food making him want to crawl out of his skin. The fear of never escaping. Then guilt walloped him, as it always did. He spoke before it drowned him. "I like being a nomad. Never feeling stuck again." He turned his face to Greg. "New Orleans is the only place I've ever come back to."

Greg cupped his cheek. "And you're not ready to stop moving yet."

Eyes closed, Tony nuzzled into the touch, savoring that too. "I don't know if I'll ever be. There's so much I was afraid I'd never get to see."

"Never taste."

"That too."

Warm lips pressed against his forehead. "Thank you," Greg said, "for coming back here. It must have been difficult."

Tony leaned in and curled a hand around Greg's neck. "But that's just it, New Orleans. It wasn't. It hasn't been." He moved his hand up, thumb tracing Greg's jaw and coasting over his soft lips. "This is so easy, at Dram and with you, and that scares the fuck out of me."

Greg covered Tony's hand with his, turned his face inward, and kissed Tony's palm. "What if I showed you it didn't have to? That you could be here and still see the world?"

Tony shook his head. "I don't—"

Greg bolted to his feet, then leaned down and stole Tony's breath with a swift, hard kiss. When he pulled back, Greg was wearing the wicked smirk that made Tony's stomach flip. "Give me one more day."

"I was planning—"

"One more day, please, baby. Take tomorrow off, then meet me at the restaurant at seven. If nothing else, let me do this as a thank you for all you've done."

Turning down that smile, turning down the chance to taste the talent that was Greg Valteau one last time was impossible. It was a risk, but one Tony was compelled to take. "All right. Tomorrow at seven."

"You need any last-minute pointers?"

Passing by the phone he'd propped against a mixing bowl, Greg shot his best friend a glare. "I did go to culinary school." He grabbed the tongs and rotated the ribs on the grill top.

"Got a hollandaise on the menu?" Miller asked.

That warranted a trip back in front of the phone and a middle finger. "Fuck you." For calling him out on his culinary devil on a night when he was nervous enough already. "And the answer is no. Just like I told Tony, I'm never putting that bitch on a menu."

Miller raised both hands in a praise pose. "Thank fuck."

Greg had to laugh, and Miller's answering smile shone bright in his beard. "Good," Miller said. "You needed that."

He did. It was the first break in tension since he'd left Tony the night before. Since this plan had come together in his head. He'd spent hours last night planning the menu, snatched a little sleep, and then today had run all over town gathering ingredients and putting it together.

He wanted the dinner to be special for Tony. Greg meant what he'd said the previous night. Even if the evening didn't go the way he wanted, he owed Tony the special meal as a thank you for the hard work he'd put into making Greg's vision for Dram a reality. But Greg sure as fuck hoped the night went the way he wanted. Except...

"I don't want to fuck this up," he said as he stirred the skillet of simmering sofrito.

"Not the kind of fucking you need to worry about tonight."

Greg rolled his eyes. "I cannot wait for you to meet some snarky twink who will turn your world upside down." There was a reason he and Miller had never hooked up. They were too much alike, and neither was the other's type.

"Says the man trying to win the heart of a hipster."

"Shut the fuck up."

Miller laughed out loud, but when he spoke again, it was with all the love and affection of the encouraging best friend Greg was lucky to have on his side. "It's a good plan, babe. Go with it."

It was a good plan, judging by the samples he tasted down the line. "It all came together." The meal, like Dram... "Because of him."

"And because you are a fabulous chef and a fabulous human being." Miller kissed the tips of his fingers and pressed them to the screen. "Now go show that boy the world."

The phone went dark, just as the guest chime beeped, signaling the front door opening and closing. Greg glanced at the front of house monitor, at Tony standing there in an outfit much like the one he'd worn the night they'd met—black jeans, dress shirt, vest. He was gorgeous, and Greg's chest tightened more than a little at the notion that this could be their last night together. Tony's reasons for being a nomad these past five years were more than valid. And if he wasn't ready to put down roots yet, or ever, then that was valid too. It would suck for Greg, but he'd have to accept it. Unless he could convince Tony he could see the world... from here.

Chapter Nine

Tony didn't know why he'd expected a candlelit two-top when he walked through the door. The set up at the bar— two simple place settings, each with a champagne flute, and nineties grunge playing through the speakers—was far more Dram's speed. The speed he and Greg had carefully crafted. Seeing the bar and place all set up, ready for critics in a few short days, for the public in a couple short weeks, Tony felt a sense of pride and accomplishment that had been missing from his other bartending gigs.

Who was he kidding?

His time here hadn't just been a gig. It had been a labor of love, on multiple counts. Which was why he'd decided to join Greg for dinner, after going round and round in his head about it all day. He'd dragged his sister onto the merry-go-round too, and it was ultimately her simple question, a variation of the same one she'd asked him a month ago—"Do you want to go to dinner, Anthony?"—that had convinced him. He'd answered the same—yes—without hesitation. He and Greg were friends, and he owed it to his friend to celebrate what they'd achieved, what they'd created.

"Grab a stool." Greg strode out of the kitchen in a stained chef's coat with a tray balanced on one hand.

Tony had seen him in the chef's coat plenty of times, but something about tonight felt different. Bigger. He made a joke to cut the tension before it strangled him. "Is there any dinner left, or is it all on your coat?"

Greg grinned, big and goofy, and pointed at a red stain midway up his torso. "This one's my favorite, but you gotta work up to that course."

Tony eyed the tray he held aloft. "Gonna tell me about that one?"

Greg's smile morphed from comical to genuine, soft and proud, and most of all, joyful. He so obviously loved feeding and serving people. "It would be my pleasure. Pull up a stool."

Tony settled in front of a place setting, and onto the square chargers, Greg set small plates with silver domes covering their contents. Tony reached out to remove the domes, but Greg's hand on his forearm stopped him.

"Drinks," Greg said. "Give me just a minute."

He expected Greg to duck into the wine closet for a bottle of champagne, which he did, but he didn't come right back to the stools. He lifted the bar flip and skirted behind the bar instead. "What are you up to, New Orleans?"

"You've put as much into Dram as I have the past month." He grabbed a shaker out of the bar fridge and gave it a few quick pumps. "I wanted to highlight my favorite contributions of yours." He opened the shaker, fitted on the strainer, and lavender, lemon, and the juniper notes of gin scented the air as Greg poured the base of Tony's Twisted French into the flutes. The first drink he'd styled for Dram. Greg topped it with champagne and garnished the drink with a spiral of lemon rind and a sprinkle of lavender leaves, just how Tony's bar bible directed.

Once Greg was back on his side of the bar and settled on the stool next to him, Tony lifted his glass for a toast. "Nicely done."

Greg turned up the music and tapped the rim of his glass against Tony's. "We're just getting started."

It wasn't a lie. Greg lifted the silver domes off the plates, revealing canapés of mornay-filled gougères, pork rillettes, and tiny truffled-grilled-cheese sandwiches. Tony might have groaned a little at his first bites. And again at the rich and light chawanmushi that followed. Steamed custard topped with gulf shrimp and radish, served with the Sake Summer, a sake, gin, and citrus concoction perfect for drinking in the hot weather.

And the medley continued. Jamón ibérico and manchego cheese croquettes, served with a Pom Fizz Paloma, the traditional Paloma recipe enhanced by pomegranate-infused club soda. Mojo chicken street tacos with Tony's own Planter's Punch, pineapple-orange juice with a spike of cranberry and aged rum. Tandoori chicken skewers with a dark rum mojito, the sweetness balancing out the spice. Drambuie-glazed baby back ribs, which were served with a perfectly mixed Balcones Bomb, one of the first drinks Tony had served Greg.

Conversation came easily, moving with the ebbs and flows of the dishes and music. Greg told Tony about each dish—its inspiration, beyond just the drink, who he'd sourced the ingredients from, when he'd first had it. And Tony came up with even more cocktail pairings, energized by Greg's cooking. While all these foods wouldn't be on the menu at the same time, owing to seasonality and scaling for a packed restaurant, it was an impressive display of Greg's range and talent as a chef and his vision for Dram. The food wasn't any one cuisine, which meant the drinks, the bar, and the place—the community it fostered—really would be the star. It was going to be fabulous.

Tony guessed, by the wide smile on Greg's face, that the dish he was carrying out next was going to be fabulous too. It was clearly his favorite, the one that had caused the stain on his chef's coat, which he'd ditched halfway through the meal. He set a bowl on each charger and an empty one between them. "My dad used to fix a version of this dish when I was a kid," he said as he circled around to the other side of the bar. "There are varieties all over the world, but this one is modeled off a Peruvian recipe. And to go with..." He pulled out another shaker, and the drink he poured was very much expected.

He'd said Peru, and drink-wise, Tony had known his watermelon pisco sour would fill their glasses. As for the dish Greg paired with it, no wonder it was his favorite. Mussels and andouille in a spicy sofrito sauce. Divine. It was definitely South American in flavor profile, but the andouille gave it a touch of New Orleans. All the dishes tonight had that same touch of Greg's hometown, while also being from around the world.

Around the world.

Tony froze, spoon halfway to his mouth, as the realization of what Greg had done tonight sunk in.

"Figured it out, huh?"

Tony glanced at Greg, whose chin rested on his chest, highlighting the slashes of pink on his cheekbones. He looked shy, embarrassed almost. Not a look Tony had frequently seen. It was so endearing it made Tony want to wrap his arms around the big man and tell him this was the sweetest thing anyone had ever done for him. And the most confusing.

Tony sipped his pisco sour as an excuse to look away, to blink back the tears stinging his eyes. By the time he lowered his glass, Greg had lifted his face, gaze equal parts hope and fear.

"I don't want to pressure you," he said. "I understand why you might not want to put down roots somewhere just yet, but I can show you the world"—he covered Tony's hand with his, pressing their joined hands together against the bar—"from right here."

Tony's gaze locked on their hands, on Greg's big one atop his more slender one, on how Greg's calloused hands had built this bar, cooked these wonderful dishes, and touched Tony with such kindness and heat.

"And we'll travel too, baby," Greg said, soft lips brushing Tony's temple. "Give me a year to get this place up and running, and then we'll go anywhere you want." He squeezed his hand, and Tony shuddered, hope and fear fighting a war inside him too. "Please, just give this, give *us*, a shot."

Leaving New York five years ago had been the scariest thing Tony had ever done. Turning his head and meeting Greg's eyes just then was the second scariest. Making a jump—a life-altering leap—always was. But he hadn't felt trapped or pressured once tonight, not even over the past month here. He'd felt... at home. *That* was what had spooked him yesterday.

It was also what gave him the courage to lean the rest of the way forward and whisper against Greg's lips, "Yes."

Greg inhaled sharply, then a wide smile bloomed on his lips. Tony captured the smile in a kiss that had them both groaning. Had Tony sliding off his stool and into Greg's arms, and Greg carrying him upstairs to the apartment above the bar.

They made it as far as Greg's bedroom wall, the plaster cool against Tony's back, the chef's body warm against his front. He wanted more of it, to touch and taste. "So this is the upstairs?" Tony teased as he worked Greg's Saints tee up and off.

"Been dying to get you up here." Greg ripped open Tony's shirt and vest, his fingers trailing through Tony's chest hair and lighting him on fire. "Best and worst four weeks of my life."

"Have I really been that bad?"

Greg nipped at his ear, his neck, his shoulder. "Working with you all the time, wanting you all the time..."

Tony smoothed his hands over the wide expanse of bare chest he'd likewise been craving. "If it makes you feel any better..." He leaned forward and ran his tongue around one puckered nipple then the other, making Greg shiver. "I've been hard this entire time too." He canted his hips and rutted his cock against Greg's abs, proving his point.

It was all the encouragement Greg needed to spin them off the wall and toward the bed, Tony ditching his own vest and shirt along the way. His back hit smooth sheets, while Greg's deliciously rough hands roamed over his skin and down to the button on his jeans. Off went Tony's pants and briefs, and Greg's hands slid under Tony's ass, cupping and kneading. "Do you have any idea how many times I wanted to bend you over that bar the past month?"

The visual, which Tony had contemplated more than a few times himself, made his dick leak and his hole quiver. "Want that too."

Greg spread his cheeks, his fingers dipping into his crease, one circling his hole. "I want to see this ass up in the air, the light streaming in through the stained glass and over your skin, while I feast on this hole."

"Ngh." He was going to explode if Greg kept saying things like that. And Greg would, if their only other night together was any indication. He'd torture and tease Tony to the very edge. Tony looked forward to that—later. He needed Greg inside him. Now. He swung a leg over Greg's head and rose up on his knees and elbows. He glanced back over his shoulder. "Fuck me here now, downstairs tomorrow."

"Fuck, you're perfect." Greg finished stripping and climbed onto the bed behind him, hands making another teasing sweep of his back and palming the globes of his ass, before reaching for the lube and condom in his bedside table.

Tony sighed with relief, then yelped as Greg, behind him once more, licked over his hole. Tony wobbled on one hand and reached down to grasp the base of his dick, staving off his orgasm. "You gotta get in me, New Orleans. Wanna come—"

"I got you, baby."

The click of the lube lid and the snap of the condom had never sounded so good. The cold dollop of lube and the burn of fingers stretching him open never felt so welcome. The pressure of a thick, hard cock pushing past his ring and inside him never so perfect. Because it was Greg.

A heavy, delicious weight settled over his back and Tony groaned his satisfaction. Warm breath coasted over his ear. "That's right, baby. Gonna make you feel good. As good as this feels to me." Greg tortured him with long, slow strokes, pulling back far enough for the tip of his cock to tease Tony's rim, then thrusting back in, all the way to the hilt. "Gonna make love to you all night long."

Tony rotated his head enough to catch Greg's heated gaze. "That's what this is, isn't it?"

"Yeah, baby, for me it is. I love you. You okay with that?"

"I think that's why I'm okay with all of this. With staying. I love you too."

Greg kissed his temple, his jaw, his lips. "I'll make it worth it, Tony, I promise."

Tony had no doubt he would. And that night he did, both of them grinding against each other, into each other, hot and sweaty, for what felt like hours. Swimming in the bliss and feeling of being at home under Greg's body, under the rough and talented hands that were clenched in Tony's each time they came together.

Sometime later, once they'd fucked themselves out, Tony rolled onto his side to face Greg, to get lost in his soulful eyes a few minutes longer before falling asleep, but his gaze skittered over Greg's shoulder to the barrel on the bedside table. "You kept it?"

Greg rolled onto his hip, bringing them chest to chest. "It reminded me of you."

"Can we have them at the bar?"

"I'd love that. You didn't add them, and I didn't want to suggest it." Greg dropped a kiss on Tony's lips and ran his fingers through his curls. "Was afraid you'd leave."

"I think maybe that's why I didn't add them. Because I didn't want to leave."

Greg grinned and hitched one of Tony's legs over his hip. "Barrel-aged Manhattan. Seems appropriate for Dram. I actually had it planned as the final drink tonight, the last drop from your barrel with a homemade cherry hand pie. But then we got distracted."

"Good distraction. And good for breakfast." Tony

hummed and snuggled closer, tucking his head under Greg's chin and sinking into sleep, and home.

Home.

"How about a barrel-aged Vieux Carré this time," he said. "Something for our bar."

Greg's laugh rumbled beneath his ear, warm, soft, and sexy. "Perfect."

Chapter Ten

"What's cooking in there?" Henry peered over Greg's shoulder, peeking into the large heavy-bottomed pot Greg was stirring on the stove.

Greg elbowed his middle. "How many drinks have you had?" If his dad didn't recognize the bright, rich smells of his own bouillabaisse—orange, saffron, fennel, fish stock—then he'd probably had one too many cocktails. But with Tony out there pouring showstoppers like the Fireside Rye, a spicy whiskey concoction perfect for winter, Greg couldn't blame his dad if he had.

"Your apartment's gonna smell for days," his dad said, drawing out the last word. Yeah, he recognized what was in the pot, all right.

"I know," Greg said dreamily. "Isn't it wonderful?" Especially the part where no one else in the building would bitch about it.

His dad squeezed his shoulder. "That's my kid."

"You want a taste of the broth?"

"Nah, I'll wait."

"Hand me the goods, then?" He jutted his chin at the bowls of cleaned and readied seafood a line cook had prepared. His dad set his glass out of the way, next to Greg's phone, quickly washed his hands, then slid in among the chefs to help. No one batted an eye, all of them used to it. Dram, more than any of Greg's other restaurants, was a family affair, in the biggest sense of the word. His parents had helped him find the place and were frequent guests. Gloria too, as were many of Dram's purveyors, especially those in the LGBTQ community. He and Tony made it a priority to seek out their business, and they returned the favor. And Greg and Tony had made it clear to each of their staff, many of whom they'd recruited from local shelters, that they were welcome to bring their friends and family here too. There were no closed doors here. Dram was his and Tony's home and a haven for their family, staff, and community. And that sense of safety, that love that started with Greg and Tony, showed in every dish Greg's kitchen put out and every drink Tony's bar served. It was everything Greg dreamed it could be, and his soul had never been happier, cooking food he was proud of, working and living with the man he loved, supporting his hometown and his community.

"Stir, son," his dad said with a nudge. "I'll get the phone."

Deep in his feels, Greg hadn't even heard it ringing.

"Hey, son." It had to be Miller. Henry only called three people "son," and two of them were here, which left only Greg's best friend across the country. "Yeah, he's here, up to his elbows in fish stew... All right, just a minute." His dad lowered the phone. "He wants to talk to you. Said it's important."

Greg yanked the hand towel off his shoulder, wiped his hands, and traded his dad the long wooden spoon for the phone. "Is everything all right?"

"Why the sudden panic?" Miller replied.

"You're calling me in the middle of service. You, of all people, know better."

"Unless that's exactly when I meant to call you." Greg could hear the sly smile in his voice. What was he up to? "Where's Tony?"

"Behind the bar."

"Get out there. Something I want to tell you both."

"Okay, hold on a second." He handed off the care of the soup to his sous, exchanged a few words with his other cooks, then headed to the dining room with his dad. Phone back to his ear, he poked at his friend. "You meet a guy?" He didn't think that would warrant a midservice call, but worth getting a dig in.

"Ha, ha."

The place was packed, but as always, Greg's attention went to the bar first. To Tony standing behind it, pouring drinks into the three highball glasses lined up in front of his mother, Cass, and his purveyor's wife, the three troublemakers no doubt scheming. It skipped on past them to... Julia? What was Tony's sister doing here? A man rose from the barstool beside her. Dressed in a flannel and jeans, his smile shone bright in his chestnut beard. Miller lowered the phone from his ear.

Greg stumbled the rest of the way behind the bar, aided by a push from his dad. "Why'd you call me if you're here?" He shifted his gaze to Julia. "And why are you here?" He looked to Tony. "Do you know what's going on?"

Tony shrugged. "No idea. They both just got here."

Greg leaned across the bar, giving Julia a peck on the cheek. "Good to see you, Jules." She and her family had visited them twice already—when they'd opened last summer and again over the holidays when Elle was out of school. "Unexpected, but a great surprise."

"Got a call from Miller and a plane ticket arrived in my inbox five minutes later. Two days later, and I still don't know what this is about. He"—she jutted a thumb at Miller —"just said I should be here and that it was a surprise."

Greg turned to Miller, ready to interrogate his best friend, but Miller beat him to it. "All will be revealed," he said with a wink, then snatched two copper mugs off the backbar and rotated toward the dining room. He banged the mugs together. "Can I have everyone's attention?" His booming voice carried over the quieting restaurant, patrons pausing midconversation to listen and Henry turning down the music with the phone he'd slipped from Greg's hand. Behind his dad, the kitchen staff were also poking their heads out to see what the commotion was about.

"You really have no idea what's going on?" Greg said to Tony.

Tony nestled against his side. "None."

Thankfully, Miller didn't make them wait any longer. "Almost two years ago," he started, "I got a call from Greg.

He sounded pitiful." He embellished the last word, and the crowd laughed. "He'd had a one-night stand with a hipster bartender, and he couldn't get the guy or his drinks out of his head."

A blushing Tony turned into Greg's shoulder, and Greg kissed his headful of dark curls.

"Turned out Greg was on to something," Miller continued. "An idea for this place and a partnership with Tony that brought them, New Orleans, and the LGBTQ community something great. Something potentially award-winning."

Tony gasped. "Holy fuck."

Greg, meanwhile, had lost all his words, the scene before him rearranging and coming back together. Realization dawning as to why his best friend and Tony's sister were here, why his family and his closest friends had all come in tonight, why his staff were gathered together and all wearing blinding smiles.

It was an occasion to celebrate.

"It is my great honor, as someone privileged to call these two men dear friends and esteemed colleagues, and as a James Beard Award winner, to share with Greg and Tony, and with you all, that Dram is a James Beard Award Finalist for Best New Restaurant and Outstanding Bar Program."

The cheers and applause were deafening, and only Tony's arms around Greg's middle held him up. "Are you serious?" Greg hollered over the noise at Miller.

Miller reached under his barstool, then laid a folder open on the bar top. He pushed it across the bar to Greg and Tony. Inside were two finalists' certificates and a pair of invitations to the awards gala. "Fourth time was the charm."

Beside him, Tony shouted, "Fuck yeah!" and the next instant, Greg's arms were full of hipster, Tony jumping up and wrapping his legs around his waist. Greg caught him by the ass, and Tony framed his face with his hands. "You did it!"

"*We* did it," Greg replied, and Tony's answering smile was brighter than all the bottles behind the bar, brighter than the sun on a hot New Orleans day, brighter than any dream Greg had ever had for this place. "*Our* bar. Thank you, Manhattan, for staying."

Tony leaned forward and brushed their lips together. "Thank you, New Orleans, for giving me the world."

Reviews are an invaluable tool when it comes to spreading the word about great reads. Please consider leaving an honest review for *The Last Drop* on your favorite review site.

Thank you for reading!

Acknowledgments

The second Greg hit the page in *Dine With Me*, I knew he had to have his own story. Thank you Leslie Copeland and Lucy Lennox, organizers of the Heart2Heart Charity Anthology, for giving me that chance and for giving me the opportunity to contribute the first edition of Greg's story to such a wonderful project. Thank you so much readers for coming back for the extended version now! Much love and gratitude to Kim for beta reading, to Susie Selva for editing, and to cover design maven Cate Ashwood, photographer Eric Battershell, and model David Lovelace for helping to complete this expanded package of NOLA-packed goodness!

Also by Layla Reyne

For the most up-to-date list of titles and a helpful reading order, please visit www.laylareyne.com.

Agents Irish and Whiskey:

Single Malt

Cask Strength

Barrel Proof

Tequila Sunrise

Blended Whiskey

Angel's Share

Fog City:

Prince of Killers

King Slayer

A New Empire

Queen's Ransom

Silent Knight

Perfect Play:

Dead Draw

Bad Bishop

King Hunt

Best Play

Standalone Stories:

What We May Be

Under the Table

Table for Two:

The Last Drop

Blue Plate Special

Over a Barrel

Changing Lanes:

Relay

Medley

Freestyle

Soul to Find:

Icarus and the Devil

Jason and the Storm

Paris and the Reaper

Atlas and the Traitor

About the Author

Layla Reyne is the author of *What We May Be* and the *Agents Irish and Whiskey, Changing Lanes,* and *Table for Two* series. She writes sexy, intense LGBTQIA+ romance featuring competent adults in kitchens, sports arenas, car chases, and other high-stakes situations. Whether it's adrenaline-fueled suspense, rival athletes, vampires and shifters in alt-realms, or love mixed with mouth-watering foodie goodness, queer folks finding happily-ever-afters is guaranteed.

You can find Layla at laylareyne.com, in her reader group on Facebook—Layla's Lushes, and at the following sites:

facebook.com/laylareyne

instagram.com/laylareyne

bookbub.com/authors/layla-reyne

tiktok.com/@laylareyne

www.ingramcontent.com/pod-product-compliance
Lightning Source LLC
Chambersburg PA
CBHW071539100726
47908CB00004B/1433